Castle in Corsica

ANNE WEALE

Originally published as Harlequin Romance #537

HARLEQUIN
CLASSIC LIBRARY

TORONTO • LONDON • LOS ANGELES • AMSTERDAM
SYDNEY • HAMBURG • PARIS • STOCKHOLM • ATHENS • TOKYO

Original hardcover edition published by
Mills & Boon Limited 1959
ISBN 0-373-80005-3

Harlequin edition first published August 1960
Golden Harlequin Library edition, Volume XIV,
published August 1971
Harlequin Classic Library edition published March 1980
Second printing November 1980

Printed in Canada

CHAPTER ONE

As SHE WAS buttoning the jacket of her pajamas, Polly thought she heard a sound from the next room. Hurriedly slipping into her dressing gown, she switched off the bedside lamp and quietly opened the communicating door. The pale radiance of the Mediterranean moonlight filtered through the filmy white curtains that screened the tall windows leading onto the balcony, and, with a sigh of relief, she saw that the occupants of the twin beds lay motionless beneath the light covers. Moving cautiously to the near bed, the thick carpet as soft as moss beneath her bare feet, she looked down at the little girl whose chubby arms were flung upward toward the ornate, gilded headboard.

In sleep, Marybelle Vanhasson's face had a cherubic innocence. When Polly had first met the chld she had been fascinated by her prettiness, her quaintly grown-up manners. Now, after five weeks of close companionship, she knew that Marybelle's pink and gold charms camouflaged traits that would be regrettable in an adult and that, in a seven-year-old, were appalling.

Perhaps, in other circumstances, the little girl's disposition might have been as attractive as her appearance, but, hopelessly spoiled from babyhood by parents who indulged her every whim but gave her no real security, she had developed into a precocious horror whose winning smiles changed to mutinous scowls or hysterical outbursts of rage the instant her wishes were thwarted. Her four-old-year brother, Vance, was equally willful, and Polly—who had always loved children and had been trained to nurse and care for them at one of the best colleges in England—wondered daily if she had any hope of taming this obstreperous pair.

With another sigh of mingled weariness and anxiety, she turned to creep back to her own smaller and less opulently furnished room. And then, on impulse, disinclined to go to sleep at an hour when most of the visitors to Cannes were setting out to enjoy themselves, she unfastened the glass doors and stole out onto the balcony.

The sky was brilliant with stars, and beyond the wide palm-shadowed esplanade and the deserted *plage* the sea shimmered under the moon, reminding her of the magnificent silver lamé gown in which Paula Vanhasson had swept off to the casino an hour ago, her ash blond hair falling in a glossy bell on her bare shoulders, her slender white arms heavy with diamond and emerald bracelets.

Dropping onto the wicker chaise longue at one end of the balcony, Polly tucked her feet beneath her, leaned back against the cushions, closed her eyes and wished that—just for twenty-four hours—she could enjoy Cannes, not as an employee with two mischievous youngsters in her charge, but as a carefree holidaymaker with nothing to do but bask on the beach, sip long cold drinks beneath a striped umbrella and laugh and chatter with people of her own age.

"Has your escort deserted you, or is the nightlife beginning to pall?"

Polly sat upright with a jerk, her wishful thoughts shattered by the alien voice. For an instant she could not think where it came from, and then, at a movement in the patch of shadow behind the couch, she twisted around and saw that a man was standing on the other side of the wrought-iron rail that divided the Vanhasson balcony from that of the neighboring suite.

"Did I frighten you? My apologies." There was a hint of amusement in the deep voice.

Polly gaped at the tall, half-hidden figure, stricken dumb, but unconsciously drawing the collar of her robe closer around her slim throat. He must, she thought, have arrived that day, because last night the suite had been occupied by another American family.

Almost all the guests were American because the hotel was too expensive for the average British visitor, but this man was not American. As he moved out of the shadow and into the moonlight, she saw that he was very dark, with crisp black hair that would have been curly were it not so closely cropped, and level black brows. But for his perfect English, which had no trace of accent, she would have taken him for a Frenchman or a Spaniard.

"You haven't answered my question," he said, looking down at her with a slight smile. "Are you alone, or do the gaming tables bore you?"

"Neither. . . I'm not here to amuse myself. I'm a children's nurse," she said coolly, beginning to recover her composure.

"I see. Does that mean you have to sit up here by yourself every night?"

"Naturally, it's part of my job."

"You don't look as if you'd been out of the nursery for very long yourself," he said. "Are you old enough to enjoy a cigarette?"

Polly flushed. She knew that out of uniform and with her fair hair released from its neat daytime knot at the back of her head, she did look considerably younger than twenty-three—but not young enough to be teased by a complete stranger. Declining the proferred cigarette with a chilly, "No, thank you," she looked away, hoping he would take the hint. But a second later, as he lit a cigarette for himself, she could not resist stealing a quick glance at him, and in the brief glow of the flame she saw that the tanned skin of his right cheek was seamed by a fine scar that extended from the temple to the line of his jaw.

An instant later she regretted the swift appraisal when he said, "Don't worry. In spite of my sinister appearance, I am not a dangerous character."

This time she flushed scarlet and was thankful for the dimness that hid the rush of color from him.

"I. . . I didn't suppose you were," she said not quite steadily.

"Perhaps not, but you obviously have doubts about the propriety of talking to strangers on balconies. If it will allay your qualms, I'll call the manager and ask him to vouch for my respectability."

"Oh, no!" Too late, she realized that he was teasing her again. "How can you tell that I am respectable? I might not be a nurse at all," she countered. "I could be a...an adventuress!"

He leaned against the balustrade, his back to the sea.

"You could. But at this hour all the shady ladies are down at the tables, and I doubt if any of them possesses that sort of dressing gown or sits around with bare feet," he said dryly.

Polly hastily tucked a fold of rose-sprigged cotton over her toes. She knew that by all the tenets of decorous behavior she ought to say a prim good-night and hurry off to bed, but something about this mocking stranger intrigued her.

"What were you thinking about just now when I disturbed you?" he asked. "Homesick?"

"Oh, no! I've always wanted to travel. That's why I took this job." She hesitated for a moment, and then admitted, "I was imagining what it would be like to come here as an ordinary holidaymaker."

"Surely you have some free time?"

"Well...no. You see the circumstances are rather unusual. There is no one to look after the children if I am off duty."

"Haven't they got a mother?"

"Yes, of course—but she isn't very strong and they are rather a rowdy pair, so—"

"In other words, she can't be bothered to cope with them," he cut in bluntly.

"Oh, no! She's very fond of them. It's just that... that some people have less knack for dealing with young children," Polly said awkwardly.

"Couldn't one of the chambermaids stand in for you?" he suggested.

"They might not be absolutely reliable. Anyway, I don't mind. We spend every morning on the beach and most afternoons we go for a drive along the coast, so I have a very good time,'' she assured him earnestly.

"How did you come to take this post?" he asked.

Later, Polly wondered what had possessed her to confide in him, but at the time it seemed quite natural to explain that the Vanhassons's American nanny had broken her leg on the first lap of their trip to Europe and they had asked a reputable London agency to find them a stand-in at the very time when Polly was waiting for a new job. Although the post with them was only a temporary one, she had jumped at the chance to travel through Europe, and if Paula Vanhasson had had any misgivings about engaging so young a nanny for her pampered offspring, the glowing terms of Polly's references and the urgency of finding a replacement for poor Nurse Harper had overruled her doubts. What Polly did not include in her brief account of the circumstances that had brought her to the Riviera was the discovery that Mrs. Vanhasson regarded paid employees as a lower form of life undeserving of any consideration or courtesy, and that Polly's position was made doubly harassing by Hector Vanhasson's persistent attempts to flirt with her when his wife was not around.

"Is the wide world coming up to your expectations?" the dark man asked, when she had finished.

"Paris did. We spent two weeks there so that Mrs. Vanhasson could get some clothes made.''

"But you're less enthusiastic about Cannes, I gather?"

Polly hugged her knees and watched a car purring softly along the esplanade before replying. "It's very artificial, isn't it?" she said at length. "Everyone is so terribly rich and elegant and. . .so *grand*. It's quite terrifying, in a way. I'm glad I've been here and seen it all, but if I were traveling by myself I think I would rather go to the smaller resorts where people are more homely and don't regard money as the most important thing in life.''

"You think people with a good deal of money are abnormal?"

"Yes, most of them. They can't help it, of course.

Being a millionaire, or practically so, must give one a distorted view, mustn't it? Although I can never understand why it has to make them quite so smug and—" she searched for the right words"—false!"

"Perhaps it's a protective device," he said casually. "They can never be sure whether they are liked for themselves or their money bags, you know."

"I suppose not, poor things," Polly said, half to herself, thinking of all the people whom she had seen around the hotel who appeared to have more than a fair share of worldly goods but whose discontented mouths and bored eyes suggested that their possessions had not brought them much happiness or serenity. It did not occur to her that the man at her side was probably one of what she mentally termed "the rich miseries."

"Have you been here before?" she asked presently.

"Yes, many times, and I share your distaste for it," he replied. "It's a pity you won't get a chance to explore farther along the coast. There are several comparatively unspoilt villages to the east where one can have good food and good bathing without so much of the tinsel overlay. Of course, the whole of the Côte d'Azur has been commercialized to some extent. One has to go south to find any real freedom from civilization."

Polly would have liked to ask him where he came from, as she was still mystified by his foreign appearance and flawless English, but, although he had questioned her freely, she hesitated to inquire about his background.

"Where are you going from here?" he asked presently.

"Through Italy, to Rome and Naples and then north again to Florence and Venice," she said, lingering over the magic names.

"Ah, Venice—the city of a hundred islands," he said. "Where, no doubt, you are hoping that some dashing Venetian will take you up the Grand Canal in a gondola."

She laughed. "There's no harm in hoping," she said lightly. "Although I'm afraid it's very unlikely."

"You would probably be even more afraid if it really happened," he said dryly.

"Why do you say that?"

"Because young women who imagine themselves in all kinds of romantic situations would almost certainly be scared out of their wits by such adventures in real life."

"I don't think so at all," Polly said, rather indignantly. "I would love to have an adventure. Lots of women lead very adventurous lives nowadays," she added.

"Oh, yes, these Amazons who cross oceans in open boats and climb mountains and hack their way through unexplored jungles," he conceded. "But they're exceptional—and not altogether admirable."

"Why not? If one admires a man for doing something brave, surely one admires a woman even more?" she said, stung by his faintly contemptuous inflexion on the words "these Amazons."

"Possibly...but I don't think women were intended to tackle feats of strength and endurance."

"I suppose you believe that a woman's place is in the home?" she said, with some asperity.

"Certainly, don't you?"

Polly drew a breath, intending to denounce this view as being ridiculously Victorian and retrogressive: realized that, in fact, she did think so and said meekly, "Well...yes, I do, as it happens."

"I thought you did. A true die-hard feminist would never make a career of looking after children. It would be much too domesticated."

She smiled. "I suppose so. All the same I don't think we are quite as scatterbrained and defenseless as we used to be—women as a whole, I mean."

He laughed. "Oh, yes, the great emancipation has had some advantages. It's much less tiresome to have a hatpin brandished in one's face than to have to deal with hysterics and fainting fits."

Below them and out of sight a car drew up outside the entrance to the hotel and a woman's voice, hard and petulant, carried upward on the still air. Thinking it might be Mrs. Vanhasson, Polly swung her feet to the floor and craned over the balcony.

"Careful! It's a longish drop."

A lean hand, dark as an Indian's against the crisp half inch of shirt cuff, reached out and gripped her firmly by the elbow.

Polly straightened, brushing back a strand of hair that had fallen across her forehad.

"I thought it might be my employers," she explained. "But it wasn't."

His hold slacked a little. "For a minute there I thought you were going to prove your point about feminine daring by pitching headfirst to the pavement. These balustrades ought to be six inches higher," he said critically.

Polly looked up at him, waiting for him to release her. She was slightly above average height but, with bare feet, the top of her head barely reached the level of his chin and the breadth of his shoulders made her feel puny. Suddenly, with his hand still on her arm, her doubts about the fitness of talking to him quickened again. But before she could pull free, his hand dropped and he stepped back and resumed his former position against the balustrade.

Polly swallowed to clear a peculiar tightness in her throat and said, stammering slightly, "I...it must be late. I'd b-better go in."

"Already?" He glanced at his watch. "It's not eleven, yet. Getting cold.?"

"Oh, no. But I think....." She hesitated, then said, "Aren't you going out?"

"Perhaps. There is no urgency."

At that moment the door on Polly's balcony opened and a small figure in a frilly nightdress appeared.

"Marybelle! What are you doing out of bed?" Polly exclaimed.

"I heard you talking," the child said, dodging Polly's outstretched hand and surveying their neighbor with interest.

"Who's he?"

Before Polly could reply, the man said, "My name is St. Clair, *mademoiselle*."

"Are you French?" Marybelle asked, climbing onto the end of the chaise longue to get a better look at him.

He shook his head.

"I guess you must be British like Polly. You talk like her."

"No, I am not British."

Polly intervened. "You've no business to get out of bed, Marybelle, and you'll get cold with no wrap on," she said hastily. "Come along."

"I don't wanna go to bed. I wanna talk to him," the child said pettishly, shaking off her hand.

"It's much too late to talk to anyone. Say good-night to Mr. St. Clair and come along, there's a good girl."

"I won't."

Polly bit her lip. She had learned that neither tactful coaxing nor firm insistence was any use when Marybelle was in a defiant mood. Much as she disliked having to use it, the only way to deal with the child was by force. So, scooping her wriggling and protesting charge under her arm, she murmured an embarrassed good-night and carried her back to the bedroom. It was inevitable that his sister's indignant howls would rouse Vance, and it was half an hour before weariness subdued them. As soon as they were safely asleep again, Polly went straight to her own bed, exhausted by the effort to keep her impatience in check when she felt certain that the one method of turning brother and sister into likable youngsters with a modicum of respect for their elders would be to give them both a sound smacking.

But although she was tired out, it was some time before she fell asleep, her thoughts returning to the rather mysterious man next door.

THE PLUMP French chambermaid who brought her a pot of tea at seven o'clock also delivered a cable from England. It was from Polly's twin brother, Andrew. He was, he informed her cryptically, in a tight spot. Could she possibly send him thirty pounds by return? The last

line of the cable read "Top secret. You're an angel.
Love, Drew."

Sipping the tea, which somehow never tasted quite the
same as it did at home, Polly wondered anxiously what
Drew's latest scrape could be. It was not the first time
that he had appealed to her to help him out of a fix.
"Top secret" meant that he did not want their parents
to find out about it.

After breakfast, Mrs. Vanhasson, who had an appointment at a beauty salon, came to collect Marybelle,
whose golden curls were the result of permanent waving
and a weekly shampoo and set. When they had gone,
Polly took Vance with her to the *bureau de poste* and
dispatched a money order to Drew's "digs" in Cam-
bridge. Fortunately she had spent very little of her
wages and was able to send the amount he had asked
for, although it meant that she would have less than a
thousand francs on which to manage for the remainder
of the week. Afterwards they went down to the beach
and Vance made sand pies. Removed from his sister's
subversive influence, he was more placid and amenable,
and Polly was grateful for a respite from the bickering
and tantrums that resulted from brother and sister being
together. She had oiled her arms and legs and was lying
on a towel, raising her head every so often to make sure
that Vance had not strayed from his pie plot, when a
voice said, "You'll be as brown as the natives in a day
or two," and, shading her eyes, she found Giles Barrington grinning down at her.

Giles was a young Englishman whom she had met on
her first morning on the beach. He had been playing
beach ball with friends and had accidentally tripped over
her feet, apologized profusely and left the game to chat.
Presently he had offered to watch over the children while
she had a swim in the deeper water beyond the paddling
reaches. The following day they had met again and very
soon were completely at ease with each other, discovering
that they were both the children of doctors, although
Polly's father was a country G.P. while Giles was the
younger son of a Harley Street specialist.

Giles himself was a medical student, at present relaxing from his studies by spending the vacation roving around the Mediterranean.

"What's new in the nursery world?" he asked, dropping down beside her, his glance lingering admiringly on her slim sun-browned legs.

Polly sat up and stretched her arms. "Nothing much. For once, all is peace and quiet," she said.

She knew that Giles was attracted to her and that, had she been free to accept, he would have asked her to dine and dance with him in the evenings. It was an annoying trick of circumstance that she would have met someone so likable at a time when the growth of friendship between them was restricted by the exigencies of her job.

"Where's The Horror this morning?" he asked.

Polly glanced quickly at Vance and gave Giles a reproving look.

"Out with mamma."

"I saw mamma when I was trying to break the bank last night. She's quite a dish, as they say in the States. Where does all the cash come from?"

"Mr. V.'s father made a fortune out of tinned ham or something," Polly said vaguely. "Mamma is one of the first Four—or is it Five—Hundred, which seems to be the equivalent of our aristocracy."

"An alliance of blue blood and ready cash, eh?" Giles said dryly. "Somehow I think Mr. V. is getting a bit cheesed off with the bargain."

"What do you mean?"

Giles shrugged. "Only that his eye was roving a good deal last night." A thought struck him and he frowned. "He hasn't made any passes at you, has he?"

Polly turned her head to hide the color in her cheeks.

"No, of course not," she said lightly, wondering if Hector Vanhasson's way of watching her and certain remarks he had made could be described as "a pass." Perhaps those discomfiting glances sideways meant nothing at all, perhaps her uneasiness whenever she was alone with him was completely unjustified.

Shaking off the momentary disquiet, she changed the

subject and they chatted companionably until it was
time to go back to the hotel.

As she put on her beach wrap, Giles said suddenly, "I
won't be seeing you tomorrow. I'm moving on."

"Oh—where to?"

"Over the border into Italy." He thrust his hands
into the pockets of his blue linen shorts and scowled at
the sand for a moment. "Look, Polly, we've got along
pretty well and this jaunt with your Americans won't
last forever. I was wondering if—when you get back to
town—I could get in touch with you, again. We might
do a theater or something."

She smiled at him. "I'd love to."

"Can I have your address?"

She gave him her address and telephone number,
which he jotted down on the back of an envelope and
tucked into his shirt pocket. Then, swinging Vance onto
his shoulders, he accompanied them back to the entrance to the hotel.

They had just crossed the esplanade when a gleaming
cream Jaguar drew up outside the hotel and a tall man
whom Polly did not instantly recognize slid out from
behind the wheel.

"Good morning, Miss Linsey."

"Oh. . .good morning, Mr. St. Clair," she said uncertainly, wondering how how he knew her surname.

"I owe you an apology," he said smoothly. "If I
hadn't spoken to you last night you would have been
saved a good deal of annoyance, I imagine."

"It wasn't your fault. Children get a bit fractious
when they're tired. Marybelle didn't mean to be rude,
I'm sure," she said regretfully.

One dark eyebrow arched skeptically and his firm
mouth tilted in a cynical smile. By daylight, his height
and breadth of shoulder were doubly noticeable and his
forearms were as dark as mahogany against the immaculate whiteness of his rolled-up shirt-sleeves. Although
the moonlight had revealed the arrogant set of his head,
the hooked nose and the forceful chin, she had taken for
granted that, in keeping with his black hair and dark

complexion, his eyes would be black or brown. Now, with a faint sense of shock, she discovered that they were vividly blue.

"All the same I feel part of the blame was mine. Perhaps I shall be able to make amends sometime," he said. And then, with a courteous nod to Giles, he turned and went up the steps into the foyer.

"What's all this about being partly to blame and making amends?" Giles asked.

"Oh, nothing really. I was sitting on the balcony last night and Mr. St. Clair spoke to me. He has the next suite. We were chatting when Marybelle came out and made one of her scenes," Polly explained.

Giles regarded her thoughtfully for a moment. "I take it you don't know who he is," he said, in an odd tone.

"Only that he's staying here and—" her eyes went to the Jaguar "—has a very impressive car."

Giles heaved Vance over his head and deposited him on the pavement.

"If you take a stroll down to the harbor this afternoon you'll see his equally impressive yacht," he said curtly. "He's got a bank balance to compete with anything in Cannes—and that's saying something."

"Has he? How do you know?" Polly asked.

"Because he was at the Casino last night and I was told about him—as much as anyone knows, that is. He likes being a mystery man, I gather. Couldn't you have brushed him off when he started being pally last night?"

"I could have done, I suppose. But there didn't seem any harm in talking for a little while. Why are you looking so disapproving?"

"Because he has the reputation of being one hell of a lady-killer. Nice girls beware!" Giles said dourly.

"Oh, I expect it's only gossip. Anyway, he'd hardly be likely to flirt with me. Men with yachts and Jaguars don't chase nannies," Polly said laughingly.

"That depends on the nanny," Giles retorted, think-ing that, even in her plain gray, uniform dress with a crisp muslin veil hiding her honey-colored hair and flat-

heeled black Oxfords on her feet, Polly was always
alluringly feminine. Just now, with her hair loose and a
cheerful yellow sailcloth smock over her brief black
swimsuit, she was worth a second glance from any man.

"If he tries to talk to you again, I would give him the
cold shoulder," he said warningly.

"Surely he can't be as dangerous as that," she said
teasingly, and then, seeing that he was genuinely concerned, "Don't worry, Giles. I won't fall for his fatal
fascination. I won't have time. We're moving on to
Italy next week, too. Perhaps we'll bump into each
other. Anyway, have a good time—and thanks for all
your baby-sitting."

She held out her hand and he took it in both of his.
"Goodbye, Polly. Take care of yourself. And don't forget, we have a date as soon as we get home."

And then, quite unexpectedly because he was not the
type to make gallant gestures, he lifted her hand and
pressed a quick kiss on the knuckles. At the corner of
the block he turned to wave and Polly waved back, feeling more than a little forlorn at having lost his cheering
companionship.

After lunch the children rested for an hour, and then
Polly dressed Marybelle in an elaborate dress of ruffled
organdy and engineered Vance's pudgy form into a
white silk shirt and green velvet shorts, because they
were going to a party at a private villa some way out of
town.

Their host came to collect them at half-past three, and
when they had gone Polly settled down in the cool of the
bedroom to mend a rip in Vance's pajamas. Paula had
intended to accompany the children but had developed
an attack of migraine during lunch and had retired to
her room. When the rear was neatly mended, Polly sat
idle for a while, thinking about Giles and wondering if
they would like each other as well in England or if their
friendship would prove to be one of those holiday ac-
quaintances that wilt in normal surroundings.

She must have fallen asleep, for when she opened her
eyes Hector Vanhasson was bending over her with a

look on his fleshy face that sent a stab of sickly panic through her.

"I. . . I'm sorry. I must have dozed off. Did you want something, Mr. Vanhasson?"

He straightened, keeping those pale, rather prominent eyes on her and grinning.

"Now there's a question," he said lazily, his drawl jarring her nerves.

Swallowing a lump in her throat, Polly stood up and attempted to pass him, but he caught her wrist.

"It must be pretty boring for you being stuck with the kids all the while."

"Oh, no! I like it."

"Aw, come off it. A pretty girl needs someone a bit livelier than a four-year-old to keep her company."

"The children *are* very lively," she said, slightly acidly. Then, trying to free her wrist, "If you don't mind, I've some things to do."

"Let 'em wait for a while." His grip tightened and he moved closer. "Are you really so cool, I wonder—"

What happened next had a nightmare quality. With a swift movement he dragged her against him, flung an arm around her waist and tried to kiss her. For an instant Polly was paralyzed by shock and disgust and then, as his hot breath fanned her cheek, she thrust both hands against his chest and pushed with her full strength. But although he ate and drank too much to be in good condition, Hector Vanhasson's strength was still superior to her own and, having gone so far, he had no intention of letting her escape without as much as a kiss. Like his children, he had always had his own way, and Polly's reserve, her brisk businesslike manner, had only succeeded in heightening his interest in her.

He had pinioned both her wrists and was deriving a sadistic pleasure from her frantic struggles, when a shrill voice from the doorway drained the amorous flush from his cheeks and left them a sickly grey. He let Polly go and turned, outwardly shamefaced, inwardly raging.

"So this is what goes on when I'm not around, is it?" Paula Vanhasson said scathingly.

SHORTLY BEFORE two o'clock on the following day, an hour when most of the visitors were still digesting their lunches and only the most ardent sun worshippers had returned to the beach to roast themselves in the dazzling heat, Polly wandered along the esplanade and wondered how she could possibly scrape together enough money to pay her fare back to England.

Her temper was still raw from the acrimonious interview that had brought her engagement with the Vanhassons to an abrupt conclusion, and she knew that any pleasant memories of Cannes would always be overshadowed by the events of the previous afternoon. Whether or not Paula Vanhasson was genuinely blind to her husband's peccadilloes, she had not hesitated to ascribe all the blame for his latest default to Polly.

At first Polly had been too shocked and repelled to defend herself, but when Paula had begun to impeach her efficiency as a nurse, her control had snapped and she had counterattacked with some trenchant home truths that had caused Paula to turn first pale with amazement and then scarlet with outraged dignity. When, finally, the American woman had scrawled a check to cover the current week's wages and an additional amount in lieu of notice, adding that she considered it her duty to write to the agency in London and advise them that Polly was not fit to be on their books, Polly had rashly torn the check into small pieces, dropped them in the wastepaper basket and walked out.

Sometime later when she counted her remaining funds and realized that she had barely enough to pay for one night's lodging in the cheapest back-street *pension,* she regretted this melodramatic but extraordinarily satisfying farewell gesture. But now, with the realization of her predicament rapidly cooling her pride, she realized that she had been a fool to let indignation override common sense.

Whatever mess Drew is in, it can't be worse than mine, she thought wretchedly. *What am I going to do?*

Earlier that morning she had been on the point of sending a cable to her father asking for enough money to cover her fare home and then, just in time, she had realized that she would have to explain why she was destitute and this would almost certainly lead to her parents finding out about Drew. Her second impulse had been to call at the British Consulate and ask for temporary aid there, but then she had remembered that such steps had a way of leading out to the press and, while she would probably be able to explain the true position to the agency, a headline in the *Daily Mirror*— "British Nursed Sacked By U.S. Society Woman: Stranded on Riviera"—would finish her career forever. If only Giles had still been in Cannes she could have asked him for help, but he was probably a hundred kilometers away by now and far out of reach.

If only I had something I could sell or pawn, she thought distractedly, wishing that she had not decided to leave her gold wristwatch—a legacy from a great-aunt—and topaz bracelet at home for fear they might be stolen or lost during the tour.

Presently, worn out by anxiety and lack of sleep, she decided to spend a few of her rapidly dwindling francs on a cup of coffee and a *croissant* in one of the pavement cafés. She was wondering if she would be reduced to swallowing her pride and asking Mrs. Vanhasson to write a second check, when a dark-haired girl in a vivid scarlet sundress came into the café and sat down at the next table. She was so attractive and so very chic that, for a moment, Polly forgot her difficulties and gazed admiringly at the girl's glossy black hair, piquant features and enviably deep tan. Suddenly the girl turned and smiled. Polly smiled back.

The girl sipped her *café noir* for some seconds, smiled again and then, rather uncertainly as if she were afraid of being snubbed, said, "You are English, aren't you?"

Polly nodded. "How could you tell?"

The girl laughed, shrugging satiny shoulders. "Oh, it is easy. You have a beautiful complexion, *mademoiselle*. What is called 'peaches and cream,' I think."

"Well, thank you. As a matter of fact I was just envying you your suntan. I don't seem to be able to get any browner than this," Polly said, looking down at her forearms, which were a warm golden color but not the almost copper shade that brunettes could achieve.

"That is because you are naturally fair while I am very dark," the girl said. "In the winter when there is no sun I am a very ugly color. Sallow, is it not?"

"Oh, I'm sure you are not," said Polly. "How well you speak English. I wish my French were as good."

"I have a spent a year in London. One must live in a country to speak its language well," said the girl. She hesitated again and then added, "Are you waiting for a friend or may I join you for a few moments?"

"Please do," Polly said.

When she had transferred her cup and settled herself comfortably, the French girl asked, "Are you alone in Cannes or with your family, perhaps?"

"No, I'm alone—unfortunately!"

"Why do you say unfortunately?"

Polly stirred her coffee. Perhaps this girl was the answer to her prayers. Perhaps she would know of a job, any job—even scrubbing floors or washing dishes—that would tide her over.

"Do you know Cannes well?" she inquired.

"Oh, yes, very well. This is the fourth year I have come here for the summer."

"Then perhaps you could advise me. That fact is, I'm in rather a spot," Polly admitted.

The girl looked puzzled. "A spot? What is that?"

"Sorry, it's a slang word for trouble," Polly said, explaining her dilemma as briefly as she could.

"But that is terrible," the girl exclaimed, with ready sympathy. "These Americans are not nice people, I think." She tapped a scarlet thumbnail against her perfect teeth and considered the situation with a contemplative frown.

"You say you do not mind washing dishes, but I do not think that would be good. The money is very small. I know! You must come to the club! There is a vacancy because one of the girls had to go home last week, and I think Monsieur Candre will give you her place if we explain.''

"The club? You mean a kind of hostel?" Polly asked.

The French girl laughed. "No, no. For two nights I stayed at your Y.W.C.A. in London. The club is not like that. Wait, I will explain. I am a student and my family is not rich, you understand, so I cannot come to the Côte d'Azur as a tourist. But I like to lie in the sun and watch all the people who *are* rich, so—'' she spread her hands "—I take work that is not too hard and earn my holiday.''

"But if you are working all day. . . ." Polly began.

"No, no, not all day. The first year I worked in a shop selling dresses to fat old women who are like sacks of flour. But that was not good because when the shop closed the sun had gone. Then last year I heard of the club and asked to work there. It is open at night, you see, so the day is free.''

"But what sort of club is it?" Polly asked.

"Like the casino, only not so big and more—" she searched for the right word "—more exclusive. Our clients are all very rich and like to play for high stakes. Sometimes they lose a fortune in a few hours, but they have so much money it does not matter to them.''

"You mean you are a croupier?" Polly said.

"Oh, no! They are always men. I am what you might call a hostess." Seeing Polly's expression, she said hastily, "It is not what you are thinking, *mademoiselle*. Everything, is very *convenable,* what you would call 'prim and proper,' I think.''

Polly regarded her gravely for a moment. She did not altogether like the idea of working in a gambling club, however exclusive, but, on the other hand, it seemed unlikely that anyone so frank and charming as the French girl could be involved in anything shady.

"I don't know. It sounds a bit out of my depth," she said doubtfully.

"But why? You are pretty and of good family. You are very well suited. Why don't you let me introduce

you to Monsieur Candre, who is the manager? Then, if
he offers you work, you can decide.''

At length, after further assurances that the club was a
most respectable establishment, Polly agreed to see
Monsieur Candre, telling herself that if there was anything peculiar about him or his premises she could easily
make some excuse for rejecting employment there.

The club was situated a short distance outside
Cannes, and while they were driving there in a taxi the
French girl, whose name was Ginette Duclos, chattered
about some of the internationally famous personalities
who had patronized it. Polly was surprised when the cab
turned into a gateway between high white walls and
drew up outside what appeared to be a private house.
Ginette asked her to wait in a cool, richly appointed hall
while she went to find Monsieur Candre and explain the
English girl's predicament. While she was away Polly
sat nervously on the edge of an elegant Louis Quinze
chair and admired the gilt-framed landscapes on the
walls.

After about ten minutes, Ginette returned and said,
''I think your troubles are finished, *ma chère.* Monsieur
Candre will see you. Don't be afraid. He is very charm-
ing.'' She led the way to the rear of the house and, with
an encouraging smile, indicated a door on the left.
''Bonne chance!'' she whispered.

Polly had expected the manager to be an elderly man,
and was considerably taken aback when, after she had
tapped at the door and been bidden to enter, the man
who greeted her with an outstretched hand and a courteous ''Good afternoon, Miss Linsey,'' proved to be
quite young and strikingly handsome in a rather flamboyant way.

''Please sit down. Do you smoke?'' he asked, offering a silver casket filled with several kinds of cigarettes.

Polly shook her head and tried not to stare at the
crimson silk dressing gown that he was wearing with a
black cravat tucked in the neck.

''You must excuse my informal dress,'' he said pleasantly. ''I was in the pool when Ginette came to find me.

She has told me your circumstances, Miss Linsey. It is a most unfortunate position, but not insuperable, I think." He paused to light a black cheroot taken from another silver box, and then continued, "As Ginette has told you, we have recently lost a member of the staff, so your misfortunes may be our good luck. That is if you do not object to working at a time when you would normally be at leisure. Our hours are from nine until two, three, perhaps four in the morning. It depends on the state of the tables, you understand. You will be provided with a suitable dress and your duties will consist of conversing with our clients, ensuring that they have all the refreshment they require and generally assisting in our aim to give the club the atmosphere of a country house party. I can assure you that the premises are conducted in a most decorous manner. We have a high reputation and are anxious to preserve it."

"It hardly sounds like work at all," Polly said cautiously.

He smiled. "It is certainly less tiring than working in a hotel kitchen, which Ginette tells me is what you had in mind. However it is not without drawbacks, I fear. Our clients are wealthy but they are not always happy. They like to discourse at length on the troubles that beset them, and to listen attentively and with patience to other people's worries is not easy. However, as you are a nurse, I am sure you are accustomed to lending a sympathetic ear. As for the salary...." He tapped his fingers on the desk for a moment and then mentioned an amount that, translated into sterling, was rather more than Polly's usual wages. "Well, what do you say?"

She hesitated. On the face of it, his offer was a gift from providence, but nevertheless she could not entirely overcome a small niggling uneasiness, a feeling that it was a shade too opportune, a shade too like what Drew would call "money for jam."

"I will tell you what I think is best under the circumstances," Monsieur Candre said, seeing her uncertainty. "Suppose you come here tonight to see how you like it.

If you find the work uncongenial, then tomorrow I will
try to assist you in finding some other work. But if you
like it here and fit in satisfactorily, then you can stay as
long as you please. If you wish to go home immediately
you have sufficient money, I will accept your decision.
But if you want to stay on for the rest of the season you
can do so. How is that?''

In the face of such a generous attitude, Polly felt it
would be churlish to refuse his suggestion without at
least giving it a trial. And, she reminded herself, with
barely the price of supper in her purse she was in no
position to quibble.

"All right, I'll have a go at it," she said decisively.
"And thank you for being so kind."

"Good. Then may I suggest that you return to your
pension and get rest in order to be fresh for the evening.
Ginette has an apartment not far from you, so she will
call for you around eight," he said. "In the meantime I
will arrange for a suitable gown to be delivered."

"How MANY hostesses are there here?" Polly asked
when, that evening, Ginette took her to an upper room
at the club where they were to change their day clothes
for the evening dresses supplied by the management.

"There are eight of us. All different nationalities,"
Ginette said, sitting down at a well-lighted dressing table
and opening a drawer filled with cosmetics. "Shall I do
your face for you? I worked in a beauty salon once. You
should wear a little eye shadow, *chérie.* Your eyes are
a lovely color, but even natural beauty can be improved
by a discreet *maquillage,* you know."

"Why, yes, if you like. Don't doll me up too much,
though," Polly said.

"Of course not. Too much paint is worse than none
at all," Ginette replied, putting a plastic cape over her
shoulders and shielding her hair with a chiffon bandeau.
She was working with deft fingers when an elderly
woman came into the room with a large dress box.

"*Voici la robe pour la demoiselle anglaise,*" she
said gruffly.

"Merci, Berthe."

"What a grim-looking person," Polly said, when the woman had withdrawn.

"Grim? Oh, you mean *très sévère?* Yes, Berthe is our chaperone," Ginette said gaily. "No, don't look at yourself. First we will put on the dress Monsieur Candre has chosen for you and then you will see how *séduisante* you can be with the right clothes and makeup."

The dress, disinterred from swathes of tissue paper, was a slim sheath of gentian-blue lace with two filmy panels of matching chiffon floating down the back from imitation sapphire buckled on the shoulders. It was an exquisite creation, and Polly could not repress a murmur of excited pleasure as Ginette lifted it carefully out of the box. But, when she had been helped into it, her excitement gave place to dismay. The narrow skirt fitted so closely that she wondered how she could possibly walk in it, let alone sit down, and the *décolletage* was very low cut.

"Oh, I can't possibly wear this, Ginette," she said.

"But why not? It looks wonderful on you. The color is perfect and lace is the right material for you. Monsieur Candre has excellent taste."

"But it's so low at the front," Polly said, blushing.

"Oh, nonsense, *petite*. You English are so prudish. You have a good figure. Why be afraid to display it?" the French girl said reasonably. "Come, look at yourself in the mirror."

Polly obeyed, and scarcely recognized herself. Somehow the blue dress and Ginette's skillful use of cosmetics had transformed her into someone quite different from her everyday self. Her eyes, delicately shadowed with silver blue paste and a narrow line of dark pencil above the lashes, looked enormous, and the cut of the dress made her figure seem more sinuous and svelte.

"You look *très élégante,* Polly. It is a pity so few young men come here. I am sure they would fall in love with you at once," Ginette said, beginning her own toilet.

Polly tried to hitch the bodice a little higher. "I don't

know. I don't think my father would approve of me looking like this," she said dubiously.

"Oh, *les parents*!" Ginette exclaimed, with an expressive movement of her shoulders. "They never approve of what their children do. It is not one's papa for whom one wishes to look pleasing."

A light tap at the door interrupted them and, drawing her satin wrap closer around her, Ginette called, *"Entrez!"*

It was the manager, his Latin good looks accentuated by immaculate evening dress. It flashed across Polly's mind that her bluff, outspoken father would probably describe him as "that damned oily gigolo."

"Ah, you are ready, Miss Linsey," he said, appraising her. "The dress is even more becoming than I had hoped. Shall we go down?"

Polly glanced at Ginette, hoping that she would suggest that they go down together, but the French girl was absorbed in applying mascara to her thick lashes.

"Ginette will join us presently," Monsieur Candre said smoothly, waiting for her to precede him into the corridor.

On the ground floor all was ready for the arrival of the first visitors. Monsieur Candre led her through three adjoining salons, each ablaze with the light from magnificent chandeliers and crystal wall sconces. Here were the "tables" that Polly had heard of but never before seen. The farthest of the three apartments was also equipped with a bar behind which two white-jacketed stewards were busily polishing glasses.

Monsieur Candre insisted that she should have a champagne cocktail, and while she was sipping it two of the other hostesses came in, one a tall blond Swedish girl and the second a vivacious Italian. They greeted Polly so cordially and politely that her persistent doubts began to ebb a little.

It was not until about eleven o'clock that the club began to get crowded. Polly, who had been standing around doing nothing up to that time, was watching a strange, raddled old woman whose sunken eyes glittered with a fanatical light as they followed the spinning roulette wheel, when Monsieur Candre came up behind her and said softly. "There is someone who is most anxious to meet you, *mademoiselle*. Come."

With a hand under her elbow, he steered her to an alcove where two men were settling down to a private game of baccarat with one of the club croupiers. Both were dark with pasty complexions and small moustaches, but while one was small and thin and insignificant, his companion, a man of about fifty, was immensely fat with heavy blue jowls and a large cigar gripped between thick pink lips. Unpleasantly, he reminded Polly of Hector Vanhasson.

"Monsieur Rodroguez", allow me to present Miss Linsey who has recently joined us," said Monsieur Candre.

The fat man eyed Polly in a way that made her stiffen, removed the cigar from his mouth and gestured for her to sit down beside him.

"A new recruit, eh?" he said with a grin that revealed several gold-capped teeth.

The manager bowed and moved away, leaving Polly to fend for herself, and it was not long before all her latent doubts about the club were being realized. The remarks that Señor Rodroguez addressed to her at intervals were civil enough, but the way he looked at her made her flesh creep, and every now and then he said something in Spanish to his friend, his great bulk heaving with throaty chuckles, while the other man shot a sly glance at Polly and tittered.

After ten minutes of this, Polly knew that she could stand it no longer and that, whatever the consequences, she could not earn her fare by making herself agreeable to such odious characters. She was mustering her courage to find Monsieur Candre and tell him this, when a waiter came to the table, bent to remove an ashtray and murmured. "There is a gentleman asking for *mademoiselle* in the foyer. It is a matter of urgency."

Polly stared at his retreating back, wondering who could want to see her. She knew no gentlemen in Cannes except her former employer, and he would scarcely seek her out after what had happened.

By now the waiter had reached the doorway to the next salon, and as she watched him, he made an almost imperceptible gesture for her to follow him. As composedly as she could manage, she asked the two South Americans to excuse her for a few moments and walked leisurely toward the adjoining room. By the time she had reached the hall the man was rearranging some glasses on his tray.

"Monsieur is in the small salon on the left," he said tersely, before moving away.

Polly walked quickly down the hall, opened the door and slipped inside. A tall dark-haired man was standing by the open window, his back to her. As the latch clicked into place, he turned and, with an involuntary mutter of astonishment, she saw that it was Mr. St. Clair.

"You!" she exclaimed blankly.

He bowed. "Good evening, Miss Linsey." Then, pulling forward a chair, he said, "Will you sit down, please."

Feeling decidedly dazed, Polly obeyed.

"I am told that you are working here as a . . . hostess," he said.

She colored. "Yes."

"Then I feel bound to tell you that, whatever brought you here, you would be wise to leave at once," he said sternly. Before she could reply he went on, "No doubt you're wondering what business it is of mine where you work?"

"Oh, no—that is, I'm beginning to realize that it was very stupid of me to come here." She paused, her head bent. "There didn't seem any alternative."

She heard him move and an instant later lean fingers tipped up her chin and she was forced to meet a penetrating scrutiny. As his glance took in the revealing dress that rode up over her knees whenever she sat down, a rush of hot, shamed color stained her cheeks.

"Very stupid indeed," he said succinctly. Then, moving back to the window, "Suppose you tell me all about it."

So, for the second time, Polly found herself confiding her situation to him. He heard her out in silence and then stood looking out into the darkened garden for so long that she was afraid he had not believed her story and was regretting whatever impulse had prompted him to warn her against the club.

"I see," he said at last. "Didn't it occur to you that the British Consulate could help you out? Rescuing travelers in distress is part of their function."

"Yes, it did. But I was afraid that if I went to them the story might get into the newspapers, and that would put an end to my career for good," she said unhappily.

"This American woman—didn't she offer you any wages in lieu of notice?"

Polly nodded. "I . . . I was too angry, too humiliated to take them."

"Well, that was natural enough, I suppose. What do you propose to do next?"

"I don't know. I can't stay here. Perhaps I can get work as a kitchen maid in one of the hotels. I've heard of people doing that."

"But not of work permits for foreign nationals, I gather," he said dryly. "No, I think there's an easier solution than toiling in a kitchen. Where are your own clothes? I assume that deplorable garment you've got on isn't your choice."

"No, it's not. My things are upstairs."

"And the rest of your gear?"

She told him the name of the *pension*.

"Mm, we can collect that later. For the moment you'd better run up and cut yourself out of that cocoon. I'll wait in the hall. Don't worry about the management. I'll settle them if they object to your rather sudden departure. What's the matter? Don't you want to get out of this very dubious establishment?"

"Oh, yes . . . yes, of course I do! Only . . ." she hesitated.

"Out with it."

She straightened her shoulders and gave him a level look.

"Mr. St. Clair, why are you offering to help me?"

A slow smile curved his mouth. "So you're wary of me now, are you?" he said sardonically. "It's a pity you weren't as cautious about your French friend's suggestion. I'm afraid you'll have to take me on trust, but if it's at all reassuring, I think I know of a better job for you, as a child's nurse. Now hurry up and change."

A quarter of an hour later, Polly sat beside him in the Jaguar and wondered if she was being utterly foolhardy to trust this man whom Giles had described as a notorious philanderer. Presently they turned onto the esplanade, but as they approached the hotel his foot did not ease off the accelerator.

"Where are we going?" she asked in surprise.

"To my yacht."

Polly stiffened. He must have sensed her sudden tension as with a note of amusement in his voice, he said, "I left the hotel this afternoon."

"Couldn't we go to my *pension*?" she said awkwardly.

"If it's as flyblown as the address suggests we shall be much more comfortable on the *Corsair*," he said. "There's no need to panic. I'm not a white-slave trader, if that's what is worrying you."

"No, of course not," she said hastily. "I just don't want to be more of a nuisance than I can help."

"Tell me, are you interested in children of a rather more advanced age than your last pair?" he asked.

"I like them at any age," she said. "Why do you ask?"

"Because the post I have in mind involves a child of nearly nine. However, we'll go into details presently. There are some arrangements to be made first."

A few minutes later they reached the quay and drew up near a large ocean-going yacht. St. Clair helped Polly out of the car and led her across the cobbles to the gangplank that was guarded by a swarthy seaman who spoke to him in what she took to be a French *patois*.

"Are you hungry?" St. Clair asked as they entered a surprisingly spacious cabin furnished as a combination of dining room and lounge.

Polly shook her head.

"All the same, I think coffee and some sandwiches might be good for morale."

He pressed a bell and another dark-skinned member of the crew appeared, took his order, bowed and withdrew.

"I've never been on a yacht before. It's almost like a house," Polly said, admiring the wide leather banquettes, the shaded wall lamps and the tweed curtains screening the portholes.

"I travel a good deal, so it has to be reasonably habitable," he said, sliding back a portion of the bleached-walnut paneling to reveal a well-stocked cocktail cabinet. "Would you care for a drink?"

She shook her head, watching him pour one for himself. The label on the bottle was one she had never seen before and she assumed it to be some uncommon variety of liqueur.

"There are two ways out of your difficulty, Miss Linsey," he said, lighting a cigarette. "Either I can lend you enough money to get home. No, don't protest. It isn't a large sum and I have every confidence in your honesty. Or you can take the post that I have in mind for the period that you intended to spend with the Americans. It might even become a permanency. Now, which do you prefer?"

Polly smoothed her skirt, thinking for a moment before replying.

"It's very kind of you to offer me a loan, Mr. St. Clair," she said, "but I would really rather earn my fare. The only drawback is that the parents of this child may not approve of me—particularly as I've just been sacked."

"Don't let that worry you," he said. "She has no parents—they were both killed in an air disaster some years ago—and I am quite sure you will be able to manage her very capably. The point is, if I make the arrangements, are you willing to accept the job, at least for the time being? I may say that the conditions of work will be considerably pleasanter than those of your previous post. You'll have a completely free hand with the child, adequate leisure and whatever salary you care to name."

"But surely whoever is responsible for her—the guardian or relatives—will want to interview me first?" she said.

"I am her guardian."

"Oh, I see. Well, in that case I should be pleased to have the job," she said.

"Right . . . then I'll collect your baggage from the *pension* and fix one or two details," he said briskly. "I won't be gone long. If there's anything you want just ring for Tonio. He speaks fairly good English. If I were you, I would snatch some sleep."

A second later he was gone.

Left to herself, Polly wandered around the cabin examining the luxurious fittings. She was looking at the titles of a row of books on a locker when the steward returned with a plate of finely cut chicken sandwiches and a pot of coffee. When he had gone back to the galley, she selected a book of short stories from the shelf, slipped off her shoes, curled up on the banquette and began to nibble one of the sandwiches. Presently she took off her jacket, and settled more comfortably against the plentiful cushions. Instead of stimulating her, the hot fragrant coffee made her feel drowsy, and, putting the book side, she decided to take her benefactor's advice and snatch a short nap.

A STRANGE SOUND roused her from the borders of sleep and she sat up, stretching her cramped legs and trying to identify the unfamiliar noise. It was a regular throbbing note like a pulse beat. She looked at her watch and discovered with a shock that it was nearly an hour since the steward had brought her the sandwiches.

And then, the icy tremor gripping her spine, Polly

knew what it was that had woken her. The yacht's engines were running.

Scrambling to her knees, she thrust aside the curtain over the nearest porthole and peered out through the thick glass. At first she could see nothing and then, cupping her hands between her temples and the pane, she saw a glittering strand of lights in the distance, lights that hung in festoons like a golden necklace. Somewhere beneath the throb of the engines grew stronger and suddenly a scatter of drops was flung up against the outside of the glass.

Only then, sick with panic, did she realize that the faraway lights were the lights of Cannes and that between them and the yacht lay a rapidly widening expanse of murky sea.

CHAPTER TWO

As THE FULL IMPACT of her situation sank in, Polly's panic gave way to an upsurge of fury—as much at her own gullibility as at the duplicity of the man who had so cleverly played the role of good Samaritan. Letting the curtain fall into place, she sank back on her heels and mentally upbraided herself for her idiocy. To have let the plausible Ginette make a fool of her was excusable, but to be duped twice within a few hours was not merely stupid but downright half-witted. How could she have been so incredibly naïve as to believe that a man whom she scarcely knew was genuinely concerned about her plight? What a simpleton he must think her! What an addle-headed little fool! Well, at least she would not add to her folly by giving way to panic. Whatever Mr. St. Clair's motive for abducting her might be, she thought angrily, he would not find her an amenable victim.

Slipping off the banquette, she put on her shoes and jacket and began to pace around the cabin, trying to think of a plan of action—or, more correctly, defense!

About ten minutes later she heard footsteps in the passageway, and in spite of her determination to maintain a cool, unruffled demeanor, her heart thudded uncomfortably. The door opened and St. Clair came in.

"Feeling better?" he asked pleasantly. "Or did the engines disturb you?"

The effrontery of this almost took Polly's breath away, and before she could reply, he went on. "I just looked in to say that we shall be having a light supper in about twenty minutes. Tonio has prepared a cabin if you'd like to freshen up. I'll show you the way."

He stood aside for her to pass through the door, but

staying where she was Polly braced her shoulders and said coldly, "I don't know whether this is your idea of a practical joke, Mr. St. Clair, but, frankly, I don't find it very amusing. Please tell your crew to put back to Cannes at once."

"Put back?" He stared at her with such an excellent imitation of genuine surprise that, two hours ago, she would have thought he was really astonished. "Why?"

Polly glanced at her watch. "It's after midnight and I've had rather a trying day," she said evenly. "The sooner we get back to Cannes, the sooner I can get some rest."

He closed the door and leaned against it, his arms folded across his chest, his expression unreadable. "D'you mean you've changed your mind about my offer?"

She forced herself to meet his glance steadily. "Don't you think the joke is wearing a little thin? I'll admit I swallowed your story if it gives you any satisfaction. Now will you please take me back to Cannes."

His eyes narrowed slightly. "I offered you a job and you accepted it. It's a little late to back out now," he said quietly.

Polly glared at him, her temper rising. "Will you or won't you take me back?" she said sharply.

He produced his cigarette case, tapped both ends of the cigarette on the lid, lit up and exhaled a thin stream of smoke. The unhurried precision of each gesture set her teeth on edge.

Then, mildly but with unmistakable finality, he said, "No, I'm afraid I won't."

In the desperate seconds that followed this conclusive refusal, Polly wondered wildly if she should have thrown a fit of hysterics the moment he entered the cabin. Perhaps her decision to appear calm and collected had been a tactical error. Perhaps screams and sobs would have served her better.

"But you must! You can't force me to stay on board," she exclaimed, her voice beginning to shake.

"Force is scarcely necessary—unless you're equal to

swimming several miles against an offshore current in the pitch dark," he said casually. "Don't look so alarmed. I don't know what dire prospects you've been imagining, but you're in no danger. Now, shall I show you your cabin?"

"Look, I don't know what possible reason you can have for doing this—" she began hotly.

He grinned. "But a most alarming possibility has obviously occurred to you."

A tide of vivid color suffused her face and throat and suddenly, for the first time in her life, she had a terrible sense of being completely powerless, utterly helpless.

"Oh, come, stop dramatizing the situation," he said easily. "You're quite safe. The days of buccaneers and captive slaves are over, my dear. This little excursion that you view with such distrust is really quite in order, I assure you. As a matter of fact I looked in to tell you that we were casting off some time ago, but you were so fast asleep that I thought it a pity to disturb you."

"How very considerate of you," Polly retorted with heavy sarcasm. "No wonder you suggested I should have a nap!"

His shoulders lifted in a shrug and then he turned and opened another panel in the wall. Behind it was a small writing desk with a light that switched on when the panel was moved. Taking something from a compartment, he turned back to face her and held out a small dagger with a thin tapering blade. "Here, take this," he said, with a smile. "Perhaps a weapon will make you feel safer. But don't cut yourself, the blade is very sharp."

She glowered at him, hating his casualness and the quizzical glint in his blue eyes. With another shrug, he snapped open her bag that she had left on the table and dropped the knife into it.

"I'm not likely to risk a second disfigurement," he said dryly, touching the scar on his cheek.

"May I ask where you're taking me?" Polly asked icily.

"To somewhere very different from Cannes, you'll be

glad to hear." He paused. "I suppose you won't believe it now, but I thought you knew where we were going."

"Oh, yes! Second sight is an essential qualification for a children's nurse!" she said scathingly.

She saw a flicker of irritation in his eyes, but when he spoke his voice was as mild as ever. "I'm sorry. I evidently miscalculated," he said. "However, since you don't know, it may as well come as a pleasant surprise."

There was a tap at the door and as the steward entered, he said, "Perhaps you would prefer Tonio to show you your quarters. I think you'll find everything you need. When you're ready for supper just ring the bell above the bunk."

There seemed no alternative but to follow the steward, and a few moments later Polly was alone again, this time in a smaller but equally luxurious cabin nearer the bow. The single rather shabby suitcase that she had brought from England had been placed on a luggage stool between the glass-topped dressing table and the built-in wardrobe. Sinking into a satin-covered armchair, she stared at herself in the long mirror clipped to the back of the door and marveled that the sequence of calamities that had overtaken her in the past forty-eight hours had left no visible mark. *Although, if this goes on, I shall be white-haired by the end of the week,* she thought with a surviving glimmer of humor.

Presently she summoned the energy to find a jar of cold cream and remove Ginette's makeup. Then she washed her face and hands at the pale yellow basin in the corner and combed her hair. The cabin was obviously designed for feminine occupation, she noticed. There was a cut glass powder bowl and an empty scent spray on the dressing table, and the lower part of the bunk was hidden by a ruffled valance of turquoise silk to match the quilted coverlet. Looking at the Redouté rose prints on the walls and the pink satin pincushion on top of the locker, she remembered Giles's warning again and wished she had considered it more seriously while she was still in the comparative safety of the Jaguar.

Her linen suit was crumpled and there was a smudge

on the skirt. After a moment's hesitation, she took it off
and changed into a freshly laundered uniform dress that
was cooler than the suit and would not give Mr. St.
Clair the impression that she had wanted to improve her
appearance.

Slipping the discarded jacket on a folding hanger, she
opened the wardrobe door and then stopped short, her
eyes widening. An evening dress hung from the metal
rail inside. Thrusting her jacket onto one of the sliding
hooks, Polly drew the dress out and examined it curiously. It had been made for someone of about the same
size as herself and carried a trace of expensive scent. Inside the boned bodice was a small silk tab bearing the
name of a leading Italian designer whose creations she
had seen photographed in the glossy magazines. Putting
it back, she shut the wardrobe door, crossed to the tall-
boy below the porthole and began opening the drawers.
The top four were empty except for some fragrant
muslin sachets, but in the bottom drawer two bikinis, a
sailcloth jacket and a pair of harlequin play pants.

Polly closed the drawer and straightened, her face
pale. So Mr. St. Clair made a habit of carrying women
passengers aboard the *Corsair* and thoughtfully provided certain adjuncts to their luggage. The inference sent a
shiver down her spine and she shot an anxious glance at
the door to see if it was lockable. Relieved she saw that
there was a stout bolt just above the handle.

Should she bolt herself in and refuse to come out until
they reached whatever port they were making for? Her
hand was on the fastening when someone knocked on
the panel and the steward's voice called *"Mademoiselle?"*

She wavered. The coffee and *croissant* with Ginette,
two or three canapés at the club and the thin chicken
sandwiches were all she had had to eat since an early
breakfast and, in spite of the late hour, she was hungry.
If she was going to have to barricade herself in, it might
be advisable to have something more substantial before-
hand. Glancing in the mirror, she saw with satisfaction
that fatigue and lack of powder and lipstick combined

to make her look her very worst. Opening the door, she followed the steward back to the main cabin.

St. Clair was reading a French newspaper when she entered. He rose at once and bowed, taking in the austere dress and her unpainted mouth.

To her vexation, he said suavely, "A great improvement, you are too young for those theatrical effects. By the way, I'm afraid we may be in for a spot of rough weather. Are you a good sailor?"

"I don't know," Polly said frigidly. "This is my first sea trip."

His mouth twitched. "Then you'd better make a good meal. If you're going to be queasy, you'll feel twice as wretched on an empty stomach."

She flashed him a glance of concentrated loathing. "What an appetizing thought!"

He grinned. "Delicacy is not my strong suit. Allow me!" With elaborate courtesy, he drew out a chair and waited for her to sit down.

Then, taking his place opposite, he said. "What part of England do you come from?"

"Berkshire—if you've ever heard of it," she said shortly.

"Oh, certainly. I have friends who live just outside Bracknell. It's a charming country." He spread his napkin. "Later on I must make a note of your address. As soon as we land I will notify your parents of your whereabouts." He paused. "What—still skeptical?"

Polly was prevented from making an acid retort by the entrance of Tonio with a tureen of savory-smelling broth. Strangely, her recent appetite had evaporated and she had to force herself to drink the soup and eat a fragment or two of crusty roll. The second course was an attractively dressed crayfish. She accepted a small helping, but when the steward went to fill her wineglass she shook her head and placed her finger over the bowl.

The man glanced questioningly at his master.

"I see you are aware of the devices by which an abductor tries to gain his sinister ends," St. Clair said sardonically. "However, in this instance your fears are groundless. The wine is merely intended to add to your enjoyment of the *langouste*. It's not particularly potent and one glass won't fuddle your wits, I assure you."

Controlling an impulse to fling the glass at his head, Polly said coldly, "Possibly not, but I would prefer some water if you don't mind."

He shrugged. "Just as you wish." Then, after instructing the steward to fetch a jug of iced water, "Aren't you afraid the mayonnaise may be drugged?"

Polly ignored this and for the next few minutes they ate in a silence broken only by the muted drone of the engines. Presently Tonio returned with the water. He poured some into the wineglass and Polly thanked him and drank a little.

Then, as she replaced it on the table, she noticed that while the glass was steady the water seemed to be tilting very slightly, first to the right, then to the left. She watched it for a moment or two and then went on eating. When after some minutes she looked again, the tilting motion was more noticeable.

Her first intimation that the "spot of rough weather" was likely to be more than a mild choppiness came when the steward had removed the salad and was bringing in the sweet. He was just closing the door behind him, balancing a tray on his other palm, when the cabin seemed to lurch sideways and he had to juggle backward and forward for a moment to save a bowl of trifle from crashing to the floor. Neither of the men seemed particularly disturbed by this, but Polly instinctively clutched at the arms of her chair and shut her eyes against the unpleasant sensation that she had sometimes experienced in the elevators of London department stores or driving at speed over hump-backed bridges.

She opened them again to find St. Clair watching her with a quizzical expression.

"Don't panic," he said easily. "The *Corsair* has weathered worse squalls then we're likely to meet tonight. She'll stand any amount of buffeting."

"I'm not panicking! It...startled me, that's all," she said indignantly.

Nevertheless, she thought it prudent to refuse the richly creamed trifle in favor of cheese and biscuits. Nothing else happened until they had reached the coffee stage, when a second sideways pitch was followed by a succession of unpleasant bouncing movements, as if the yacht were being slapped from below by a giant hand. This time Polly felt her inside contract and was amazed at the calm way in which Tonio went about clearing the table, keeping his stocky legs slack at the knee so that his balance was unaffected.

The next ten minutes were increasingly alarming. She had supposed that a fair-sized yacht would weather even a severe storm with little or no disturbance, but very soon she realized that, subject to the tremendous forces of nature, the *Corsair* was almost as puny as a motor launch. The throb of the engines was lost in the roar of the gale and the walls of the cabin seemed visibly to quiver against the violent onslaught of the waves outside. The reason for so many of the fitments being enclosed by panels was now all too apparent and, as the yacht began to pitch more steeply, St. Clair put away several heavy glass ashtrays and other loose impedimenta.

Polly sat with her feet braced against the heaving floor, willing herself not to be ill. Storms were like horses, she told herself firmly. One had only to accustom oneself to their movements and all was well. The trouble was that, unlike a horse, the yacht did not rock in one direction only.

"Feeling all right?" St. Clair asked, keeping himself steady with the same loose-jointed swaying stance as the steward.

Polly nodded, swallowing a constriction in her throat. "Won't we be blown off our course?" she asked, having to raise her voice against the howl of the wind.

"Could be." He grinned. "We may even find ourselves back in Cannes. I think I'd better go up and see what's going on."

"Oh, no! Please. . .!"

Involuntarily, she sprang up and clutched his arm. At

the same instant the yacht gave a violent plunge and she
was flung against him. For a second she thought they
would both fall headlong, but he had evidently anticipated the upheaval and stood firm, holding her by the
shoulders.

"It's going to be rougher than I thought. You'd better get on your bunk. It's less noticeable lying down."

Polly lifted a hand to her spinning head and felt an
hysterical urge to scream with laughter. That any position could reduce this ghastly turmoil was beyond belief.
Without waiting for her assent, he opened the door,
secured it by some means that she was too dizzy to notice,
took a firm grasp of her upper arm and half pushed, half
hauled her along the passage to the other cabin.

When they reached it, he said, "Now lie down and try
taking deep breaths. I'm going up to the wheelhouse. I
won't be long and Tonio is next door, so you'll be perfectly safe. This rumpus won't last long."

Ten seconds later she was thankful for his absence
when, as she clung to the dressing table to steady
herself, a terrible wave of nausea swept over her and she
had only just time to reach the basin before she was
briefly but exhaustingly sick.

When—how much later, she had no idea—St. Clair
came back, she was kneeling against the armchair feeling that it would be better for the yacht to sink than to
endure this misery much longer. She was only hazily
conscious of what followed: dimly aware of being lifted
onto the bunk, of having her shoes and dress removed
and being forced to swallow some vile-tasting draft.
Then everything faced into the dark haze of prostration.

WHEN POLLY AWOKE from the heavy dreamless sleep of
exhaustion, it was daylight and a shaft of golden sun-
shine was pouring through the porthole. For a while she
lay very still, afraid that at any second that racking
sickness would overtake her again. Presently hardly daring to believe it, she realized that the yacht was no
longer pitching and rolling on a violent sea. The storm
was over.

A faint rustling sound made her turn her head and she saw that the port had been opened and a light breeze was stirring the curtains. Slowly and cautiously she lifted her head.

Then, after waiting a moment to make sure that she was not going to be dizzy again, she raised herself into a sitting position. She had been sitting up for some minutes, content to enjoy this blessed return to normality, when there was a knock at the door. Hastily pulling the bedclothes up to her chin, she called, "Come in."

"Good morning. Feeling better?" St. Clair asked, closing the door behind him and setting a tray on the locker.

"Yes, thank you."

He eyed her searchingly for a moment and then said, "Where's your dressing gown? In your case?"

Polly nodded and watched him open the suitcase, remove some shoes and blouses and find her housecoat. He tossed it onto the bed and turned his back while she put it on.

"How's your appetite?" he asked presently, grinning at the expression of revulsion on her face at the mention of food. "All the same you must get something down. An empty inside only prolongs the agony. Here, try this."

He handed her a beaker with a hot, thick yellow brown concoction. Polly looked at it, shuddered, and turned her face away.

"I really don't want anything, yet," she said weakly.

"You must have some nourishment."

"No, please, I couldn't possibly."

"Drink it!" The clipped tone warned her that his patience was dwindling.

Inwardly seething with resentment but still too worn and shaken to muster defiance, she took the cup. "What is it?"

"Brodetta. An excellent remedy for everything from seasickness to lumbago. Hold your nose if it will help."

Mentally adding the obnoxious-looking potion to his list of crimes, Polly shut her eyes, tried not to inhale the rich aroma assailing her nostrils, and forced the mixture down in two or three rapid gulps. Surprisingly, it tasted much better than it looked.

"Good girl. There's nothing like strong coffee with a couple of eggs beaten into it for soothing one's innards," he said cheerfully. "Now try one of these wafer biscuits."

This time she obeyed without demur, and by the time she had finished the wafer the gnawing ache inside her had begun to lessen and she was sufficently recovered to be conscious that she must be looking a fright. Apparently unaware that a woman's first instinct after surviving any kind of ordeal is to put her appearance to rights, St. Clair sat down in the armchair, crossed long legs and said, "It was a pity your first trip had to be a rough one. If I had known the squall was blowing up I would have postponed our sailing. Never mind, I expect you'll have forgotten all about it by tonight."

Polly was tempted to retort that only a permanent state of amnesia could blot the events of the night from her mind, but she held her tongue, merely asking him in an expressionless tone of voice if he had felt no ill effects himself. He was, she noticed, wearing a blue cotton shirt and khaki slacks, and somehow the casual garments made him look younger and less autocratic.

"No, I come from seafaring stock. I'm used to rough weather," he said carelessly. "You would probably have been all right yourself if you hadn't been so strung up to begin with."

"Oh! Of all the insufferably smug, self-satisfied, egotistical...!" Words failed her and she sat glaring at him, her fists clenched with the force of her indignation.

He grinned. "You should learn Italian. It's the best language in the world for fine abusive phrases. Remind me to teach you a few when we have a spare moment."

Polly almost choked with fury. "We won't have any. The minute I get off this horrible boat I'm going straight home to England, and I hope I never set foot out of it again," she exclaimed fiercely.

"Oh, come, don't tell me you've lost your thirst for

travel and adventure already." He paused, looking toward the port. "Take a deep breath and tell me if you notice anything," he said.

Still stiff with impotent rage, she sniffed.

"Only a seaweedy smell," she said ungraciously and then sniffed again, her forehead wrinkling.

"Caught it?" he asked, watching her.

Reluctant to agree with him on anything, but puzzled and interested, she nodded, trying to define the curious fragrance that mingled with the salty tang of the breeze.

"What is it?"

An odd smile curved his mouth. "It's the *maquis*," he said. "We are nearly there." An instant later he had gone.

As soon as the door closed, Polly scrambled out of the bunk and hurried to the port. But there was nothing to see but a limitless expanse of sunlit sea beneath a cloudless sky. Impatient to discover what he had meant by his last remark, she bolted the door, threw off her housecoat and underclothes and began to wash. All the while she was dressing, the strange wind-borne scent grew stronger.

At last, trim and slender in a white blouse and flowered cotton skirt, she stepped out into the passage and walked toward the narrow companionway leading upward.

"I thought you'd be in a hurry to see where you're going," St. Clair said, meeting her at the top of the steps.

At first the sunlight was so brilliant that she was dazzled. Then her vision cleared and with an indrawn breath of astonishment and wonder she found that on the port side, they were quite close to land.

"Well? What do you think of it?" he asked, close behind her.

She gazed spellbound at the line of massive cliffs skirted by a ribbon of white beach that lay less than a mile inshore. Cliffs of sun-gilded rock, rearing like the bastions of some fairy tale fortress with tall gale-twisted pine trees growing on their summits.

"It's...beautiful!" she said at last. "But where are we?"

He took her arm and led her to the rail.

"Your education has been sadly neglected, Miss Linsey," he said dryly. "We're approximately a hundred miles southeast of Cannes. Those are the cliffs of Corsica."

CHAPTER THREE

."CORSICA!" SHE EXCLAIMED bewilderedly. "But—"

"Don't tell me you've never heard of it," he put in dryly.

"Oh, yes—I've heard of it," she said blankly, trying to remember exactly what she had heard. "But I thought we were going farther along the Riviera toward Italy. Do you mean that you are a . . . a Corsican?"

He nodded, amused by her expression. "What did you think I was?"

She made a small baffled gesture. "I . . . I wasn't certain. A mixture, I suppose." Then, afraid this might anger him she added hastily, "You speak English so well and . . . and your eyes are blue."

He shrugged. "There are always exceptions to the rule. Some Italians are fair and I know a Spaniard with red hair. Haven't you met any Englishmen with black hair and brown eyes?"

"Well, yes—but somehow one thinks of Corsicans as being very dark."

"With flashing eyes and fierce mustaches, I suppose," he said with a tinge of satire. "Frankly I doubt if you've ever given us much thought."

"I'm certainly not likely to forget about you in future," Polly replied frostily, uncertain whether the discovery of their destination was a relief or an added anxiety. Vague recollections of having heard the island described as a desolate and lawless place whose inhabitants lived in a most primitive fashion and engaged in blood feuds stirred her memory.

But her sharp retort succeeded only in making St. Clair laugh and after a moment he said easily, "You were right in thinking me a mixture, as you put it. I'm

Corsican by birth and inclination, but my accent and my eyes are a legacy from my father who was not an islander.''

Polly waited for him to go on, but he paused, obviously enjoying her patent curiosity.

"I'm sure it will reassure you to learn that the hot blood of my savage Corsican forebears is diluted with some of your own ice water," he said unkindly.

"Your father was English?"

"Yes, but not in the best tradition, I'm afraid. He never got along with his family, and after he married my mother they disowned him altogether."

"And your mother's people? Did they approve of her marrying him?" Polly asked, too much interested to remember the need for repressive hauteur.

"They weren't alive to object, and if they had been I doubt if she'd have paid much attention to them," he said. "She was a willful creature until my father tamed her, I'm told." He looked away toward the towering cliffs and without expression said, "They were both drowned in a storm when I was a schoolboy."

"I'm sorry," Polly said quietly.

He glanced at her, one dark brow arched. "Are you? Why? I thought you heartily detested me?"

"I'd be very inhuman to be glad you'd lost your parents, whatever else I may feel," she said stiffly.

"You take it for granted that the lack of parents is a loss," he said. "Is your family such a happy one?"

She ran her fingertips along the white-painted rail, controlling a sudden quiver of her lips. "Yes, very happy," she said, a little huskily.

"So they would be worried if they knew what had become of you?"

"Naturally."

He watched her speculatively for a moment or two and then said abruptly, "Don't look so forlorn, my dear. You'll see them again. Now, if you'll excuse me for half an hour, I must have a word with the skipper."

When he had gone, Polly leaned her arms on the rail and gazed down at the foam creaming past the bows and spreading into a tossing white wake behind them. Presently her gaze lifted to the cliffs and she concentrated on recalling everything that she had ever heard or read about Corsica. The total was not very enlightening. All she could remember was that Napoleon Bonaparte had been born there and was quoted as saying that he would know the island with his eyes closed because of the strange scent of the *maquis* on the hills; that it was a department of France, and that the sanitation was said to be appalling.

She was still deep in speculation when St. Clair came back, startling her because the faded espadrilles on his feet made no sound on the sun-bleached deck.

"Another half an hour and we shall be there," he said. "Come below and have a homegrown apéritif to sharpen your appetite."

This time Polly accepted his suggestion without demur. While he was pouring wine into two glasses, she said, "May I ask how you are going to take me ashore?"

He handed her one of the glasses. "So the fact that I am half English hasn't entirely dispelled your fears?" he countered.

"Did you think it would?"

He lit a cigarette. "It won't be necessary to smuggle you through customs, if that's what you're thinking. We are not putting into a port, but even if we were I doubt if you would shout for help."

"You underestimate me," she said coldly.

"I don't think so. In my experience the English never make a scene unless they are sure of their ground," he said negligently. "And you aren't sure, are you?"

Polly's chin lifted. "I'm sure that this...this whole extraordinary business has gone quite far enough and that I've no intention of putting up with it for a minute longer than I can help," she said firmly.

He smiled. "You won't have to." Then he said, glancing at his watch. "A little while from now you'll probably be most contrite for having harbored such base suspicions about me."

"As you said a little while ago, there are always exceptions to the rule, Mr. St. Clair,'' she retorted. ''I wouldn't advise you to count on my being as compliant as your previous 'guests.'''

''My previous guests?'' He eyed her oddly. ''What d'you mean by that exactly?''

She gave him a scornful glance. ''Some of the contents of my cabin are rather a giveaway, don't you think?''

His eyebrows contracted for an instant and then to her fury, he grinned. ''Well, well. For a delicately nurtured English miss you have a nastily suspicious mind. So you found some women's clothes and deduced that I'm in the habit of carrying hapless young women to my, er, stronghold, did you?''

Something in his tone made her flush. ''What would you think if you found a man's clothes in a single girl's flat?'' she demanded.

''I doubt if I would jump to such a damaging conclusion on such shaky evidence,'' he replied dryly. ''Sorry to disappoint you, but the stuff in your cabin belongs to Nicole—my sister.''

''Do you really expect me to swallow that?'' Polly said scathingly.

He shrugged. ''It makes no odds. If you prefer to think the worst, go ahead.''

''What else can I think?'' she said fiercely.

His mouth hardened. ''You might stop flattering yourself that you're capable of driving me to such extraordinary lengths,'' he said crisply, moving forward to replenish her glass.

Polly's cheeks crimsoned and her hand flew to her face, a characteristic mannerism whenever she was angry or distressed. He must have misjudged the movement, for as her arm lifted strong fingers snapped around her wrist.

''I wouldn't if I were you,'' he said softly. ''I might be tempted to retaliate in a way in keeping with your charming suppositions.''

She tried to wrench free. ''Let me go!''

Neither of them had heard a tap at the door, but when

it opened and the steward came in, St. Clair's grasp slackened and he stepped back a pace. "Well? What is it?" he asked curtly.

The man said something unintelligible and ducked out again, but not before his bird-bright eyes had taken in Polly's rebellious face and cradled wrist. As he closed the door his teeth flashed in a broad grin.

For some seconds after he had gone St. Clair stood frowning after him. Then without expression, he said, "You'd better get your things together. We are nearly there," and left the cabin.

When, having repacked her case and put it outside her cabin, Polly went on deck again, the yacht was closer to the coast, close enough for her to see that the steep sides of the cliffs were misted with great feathery clumps of rock plants. And then for the second time that morning, she caught her breath in wonder. Not far ahead lay a wide bay on the far side of which was a great promontory that blocked the view of the coastline beyond it. And on the highest point of this massive outcrop, looking at first sight as if it were some fantastic rock form, stood an ancient castle.

Presently, as the yacht altered course and swung across the mouth of the bay, she saw that a wooden jetty had been built out from the rocks and on it a group of children were jumping up and down and waving excitedly. Somehow the sight of the small eager figures gave her fresh courage.

St. Clair did not appear on deck until the *Corsair* was edging gently into the jetty, and then when a couple of rough-looking men had secured the mooring ropes and put a gangplank in place, he said briefly, "Follow me, please. Tonio will bring your bag up," and led the way onto the jetty where the children bounded around his long legs like so many scruffy but abundantly healthy puppies.

Walking behind and watching him toss packets of sweets into their outstretched hands, she wondered if this show of benevolence was for her benefit—and then felt oddly ashamed because it was obvious that they all adored him. The castle now towered above them, reached by a winding flight of several hundred steps and a strange contraption like a long metal slide with cables running up it. Near the cliff face the children pelted off toward the steps and began scrambling up them, all except a small mop-haired boy in a pair of raggedy shorts that were several sizes too big for him. At the foot of the slide was a kind of large box with glass windows and an iron grille across the front. Swinging the boy onto his shoulder, St. Clair pushed back the grille and gestured for Polly to step inside. A moment later, at the touch of a lever, the three of them were being hauled slowly up the cliff.

It took several minutes to reach the top, and when the cage cranked to a standstill Polly found that they were level with a broad flagged terrace guarded by a high stone balustrade. Still carrying the child, St. Clair reversed the lever and set the lift creaking downward again. Then without glancing at Polly, he strode across the terrace and around a corner toward the other side of the building. From the bay the castle had seemed to be perched on a narrow ledge with no access other than by the way they had come. But on the south side the promontory broadened, and as they passed under a narrow archway Polly's eyes widened, for here the bleak north terrace gave place to a magnificent garden cut by a wide graveled driveway leading inland through a screen of trees. And above the trees were the distant peaks of mountains.

She was so busy taking all this in that it was not until St. Clair set the boy down and set him scampering off to rejoin his brothers and sisters that she found they had reached the castle's main entrance, a massive stone doorway at the top of a flight of steps.

St. Clair looked at her, his face unreadable. Then with a faintly derisive smile, he bowed and said, "Welcome to Castel Maranza, Miss Linsey."

Afterward Polly wondered if she would have refused to go into the castle had they not been interrupted. But as she stood at the foot of steps, hesitant and wary, a wizened old woman in a long black dress suddenly appeared in the doorway and began speaking in an urgent and querulous tone to St. Clair.

"Mm, it seems that your arrival is even more opportune than I anticipated," he said when the old woman had finished. "Marisa is ill. We had better take a look at her at once. This way, please." And taking Polly's arm, he led her through the doorway and into the building.

With the old woman hobbling hurriedly ahead of them, they crossed a lofty hall, climbed a staircase and passed through a succession of dim corridors until they reached a doorway almost as large and ornate as the entrance.

Here, the woman stood aside and St. Clair pushed opened the double doors and gestured for Polly to enter. The room within was darkened and shadowy, but when her eyes adjusted to the meager light she saw that it was dominated by an enormous four-poster bed with a heavy canopy and rich draperies.

Behind her, St. Clair crossed to the tall windows and thrust back the curtains letting in the sunlight. The room sprang to life: a wide lofty apartment with a gilded ceiling, handsome antique furnishings and a thick pile carpet. But Polly was not aware of these details. She was staring at the bed, in the center of which, her head and shoulders propped up by a mound of embroidered and lace-trimmed pillows, lay a small girl about eight or nine years old. Her eyes were closed and her bony little hands lay lax on the sheet, but her sleep was not peaceful. As they drew nearer she began to toss restlessly and murmur broken phrases.

"What is it? Is she delirious?" St. Clair asked in an anxious undertone.

Polly studied the child's face that, although beaded with moisture, was not flushed with fever.

"I don't think so. I believe she's having a nightmare," she said quietly.

Even as she spoke the child's voice rose to a frantic wail and then, thrusting off the heavy bedclothes, she gave a strangled squeal of terror and shot bolt upright, her eyes opening, the pupils dilated with fear.

Polly did not wait for the other two to react. Tossing her bag onto a chair, she bent quickly over the bed, put her arms round the quivering little body and began to murmur gentle reassurances.

"Don't cry, dear. It was only a nasty dream. You're quite safe now."

At last the child's convulsive sobs slackened and, sufficiently recovered to realize that the comforting arms around her and the quiet steadying voice were not familiar, she raised a tear-stained face and blinked bewilderedly at the stranger.

"Better now?" Polly asked with a smile, smoothing back a wing of thick black hair that was falling over the little girl's damp forehead. She had no idea whether the child spoke any English, but knew from experience that children, like animals, were quick to understand a tone of voice.

Somewhat to her surprise, the little girl drew a long quivery breath and then, with only a slight trace of accent, said, "Yes, thank you. Who are you?"

"This is Miss Linsey, who is going to look after you," St. Clair said before Polly could reply.

He had been standing behind her, and now, seeing him for the first time, the child gave a shriek of delight, scrambled to her feet and flung herself into his arms, pouring out a flood of excited questions until a fit of coughing cut her short.

"What's all this that Renata tells me about you being ill?" he said, pushing a handkerchief into her scrawny little hands. "You shouldn't be prancing around in your nightdress, young woman. No wonder you get these chills. Back you go, *petite,* or Miss Linsey will think she has a hooligan on her hands."

With reluctant obedience the child slid down the bed and submitted to being tucked in. "Why didn't Renata tell me you were coming?" she asked.

"She didn't know. It's a surprise. Aren't you pleased?" he asked with a twinkle.

"Oh, yes! It's a lovely surprise—if you're going to stay," she added doubtfully.

"I think so, for a week or two at any rate. Now, it's time you were properly introduced. Miss Linsey, this is Marisa St. Cyr, my niece and ward. Marisa, this is Miss Linsey who comes from England."

With quaint formality the little girl held out her hand and said, "How do you do. Welcome to Castel Maranza."

"Thank you, Marisa. Perhaps when your cold is better you'll show me around," Polly said warmly, thinking how very different this polite biddable youngster was from the Vanhasson offspring. Now that her tears were dry and pleasure at seeing her uncle had brought a sparkle to her large dark eyes, one could see that, although she was not a pretty child, she had considerable charm. They chatted for some minutes until St. Clair said it was time to show Polly her quarters so that she could unpack before lunch.

"And you must keep warm and rest, baggage," he said to his niece. "Renata will be bringing your lunch up in a moment, I expect."

At the mention of the old housekeeper, a strange expression crossed the child's face and Polly noticed that her lower lip quivered slightly. *I believe she is afraid of her,* she thought. *No wonder, poor baby. The old woman may mean well, but her appearance is enough to frighten anyone.*

Aloud, she said, "I expect it's dull for you being kept in bed. If you like I'll come and tell you a story before you have your afternoon nap."

"Oh, *please.* Will you really?" Marisa said eagerly.

"Of course, see you later."

At the door she looked back for a moment, her heart quickening toward the lonely little figure in the great curtained bed. And as she followed St. Clair along another passage, she wondered why, when the child was well and even lavishly cared for, she was so thin and peaky. The voluminous folds of the old-fashioned pin-

tucked nightdress had not concealed the spindliness of
her body, and for a youngster who lived in a country of
almost perpetual sunlight she was markedly pale.

Presently St. Clair showed her into an apartment
similar to the one they had just left

"This room overlooks the sea. If you find the sound
of it disturbing we can transfer you to the other wing
tomorrow, but the rooms there aren't used a great deal
and will need airing," he said, glancing around to see
that everything was in order.

Polly looked at the gaunt stone walls hung with
lengths of tapestry and gloomy oil paintings. It was the
atmosphere and not the temperature of the room that
made her shiver.

"What's the matter?"

"N-nothing." she hesitated and then said, "This is all
rather formidable to someone used to small English
houses."

"Is it?" He looked amused. "I expect you'll soon get
used to it. Aren't you pleased to find that my reason for
bringing you here is genuine?"

She turned away from him. "You had no right to tell
Marisa I had come to look after her."

"Don't you like her?"

"She seems a delightful child. That isn't the issue."

"You mean that I am the fly in the ointment," he said
dryly. "All the same I hope that you'll be able to
overcome—or, at least, stifle—your dislike of me for
her benefit. She badly needs someone young and
modern to take care of her. Old Renata does her best,
but she's over sixty and very set in her ways."

"Is there nowhere else she could go? No other relatives who have children of their own?" Polly asked.

"Unfortunately not. If she were strong I would send
her to a good boarding school in France or England, but
I don't think she's up to it at present."

"No, certainly not, she's much too high strung to
cope with community life," Polly said. "Has she always
been delicate?"

"It's hard to say. She has a lot of colds and chills that

send Renata into a panic, but I got a first-class doctor to look her over and he said that there was nothing seriously wrong. It may be some kind of nervous trouble resulting from her parents' death.''

"She asked if you were staying. Are you away a great deal?" Polly asked.

"Yes, a fair amount. I have business interests in France." He paused. "Well, what are you going to do? If you want to go straight home, I won't stop you. Or have you the pluck to give it a trial?"

Polly met his eyes steadily. "You can't 'dare' me into staying, Mr. St. Clair," she said. "I'll have think about it, and the answer will most probably be 'no.' ''

He shrugged. "Very well. Lunch will be ready whenever you are.''

"If you don't mind I should prefer a tray up here. I'd like to be alone for a while," she said stiffly.

"By all means." He bowed, turned on his heel and left the room.

AROUND SIX O'CLOCK Polly was leaning out of the window watching the sea when she heard shuffling footsteps in the corridor and presently someone knocked at the door. It was the old housekeeper bringing a note.

Knowing that Renata was watching her closely, and wondering if she resented her arrival, Polly unfolded the sheet of paper and read: "I am dining at seven. Please tell Renata if you will join me or if you prefer to eat alone. R. St. C.''

Pocketing the message, Polly said, "Thank you, Renata. Will you tell Mr. St. Clair that I will join him for dinner, please.''

The old woman nodded and departed.

When she had gone, Polly went into the bathroom adjoining her room—the castle might be furnished with heirlooms, but there was nothing antique about the plumbing she had discovered—and ran a lukewarm bath. After lunch she had carried out her promise to tell Marisa a story, and later, when the little girl had dozed off, she had returned to her bedroom and lain on the bed for an hour, wrestling with uncertainty. At half-past four a plump country-cheeked maid who spoke no English had brought her a tray of tea and thin bread and butter.

Now, lathering her arms and shoulders, she was still undecided about what to say to Mr. St. Clair. She remembered a remark he had made on the yacht. *"The English never make a scene unless they are sure of their ground. And you aren't sure, are you?"* Was that true? Had there been any time on the yacht when she had been really frightened of him? Facing the question honestly, she knew that there had not. Oh, she had been panicky and outraged and angry—yes. But never really terrified, never absolutely convinced that his attitude was not a calculated pose. Yet why not? *Why not,* she asked herself. Because he was not visibly coarse and dissipated like that awful South American man at the club? Because his face did not seem the face of a man without scruples or consideration?

She could not find an answer and shrugging that aspect of the problem aside began to consider the child, poor mite. He had been right when he said she needed someone young and modern to look after her. If she wasn't taken in hand pretty soon, she would grow up to be scared of her own shadow. That bedroom was half the trouble. No highly strung overimaginative child should be made to sleep in a room full of shadows and creaks, miles away from the rest of the household.

Before she realized it, Polly was planning how best to bolster Marisa's diminished morale, all her professional instincts coming to the fore. Children who were suffering some form of neglect were always the most challenging and rewarding cases.

It was a quarter to seven by the time she had changed into a full-skirted dress of rose and white cotton and applied matching lipstick. Slipping her feet into a pair of white calf pumps, she fastened a single strand of chain store pearls around her neck, tucked a clean handkerchief into her pocket and set out to find the way downstairs.

It took her some time to find her way through the labyrinth of passages to the main staircase—there were several narrower flights in various parts of the castle—and as she walked down into the large hallway, St. Clair appeared at a doorway and said, "I was about to come and fetch you. People tend to lose their way until they grasp the layout."

"I was wondering if I ought to leave a paper trail to mark my way back," Polly said with a faint smile, pausing on the threshold of what appeared to be a very grandly appointed living room.

"What would you like to drink?" St. Clair asked. "Sherry, Cap Corse, tomato juice...?"'

"What is Cap Corse?" she asked.

"You had some this morning before docked. It's our equivalent of an Englishman's mild and bitter."

"Just a little, then, thank you." She sat down on one end of a couch and looked around her. Unlike the bare stone walls in the other rooms she had seen, the salon was hung from floor to ceiling with rich ivory damask and close-carpeted with a deeper ivory pile overlaid in places with Oriental rugs that had worn thin with years, perhaps centuries, of use, but that were still beautiful in their muted colorings. All the furniture was French and genuine eighteenth century, she guessed, but two large five-seater couches covered with dark green silk in the center of the room were obviously modern, although they blended surprisingly well with the tone of the room.

Dinner was served at a small table on the terrace beyond the salon, and during the meal that concluded with strong black coffee in fragile Limoges cups and glasses of Cédratine, a national liqueur, St. Clair put himself out to be an attentive and amusing host. As she might have guessed, he had traveled all over the world from Valparaiso to Afghanistan and, rather unwillingly, she had to laugh at his droll anecdotes.

It was not until they returned to the salon and Tonio, who apparently joined the indoor staff when the yacht was not in use, had withdrawn that he said, "Well? Do you want me to drive you down to Ajaccio tomorrow to catch the noon plane, or are you going to risk it for a week or two?''

She traced the pattern on her skirt. ''What will you do about Marisa if I leave?''

His shoulders lifted. ''Try to get hold of someone else. Unfortunately most of your colleagues seem to want television or radio or at least a convenient cinema to brighten their leisure. Not unnaturally, I suppose. We live very simply here and it's not very lively for an outsider.'' He smiled at her, and she was aware that when he chose to exert it, his charm was dangerously disarming. ''Having brought you here under duress, as I suppose you regard it, I had better point out the drawbacks.''

She met his blue eyes gravely, her hands trembling slightly at the moment of decision. ''Very well, Mr. St. Clair, I'll give it a trial,'' she said steadily. ''But on two conditions, one that I have a completely free hand with Marisa and, secondly, that you let me leave whenever I choose.''

He inclined his head. ''For what it's worth to you, you have my word on both.''

There was a small silence. ''You don't seem at all surprised,'' she said at length.

''I'm not. I knew you would stay.''

''Oh? How?'' she said, a shade indignantly.

''Because, as you told me when we first met, you've always wanted an adventure, and because you asked Marisa to show you around when she was better,'' he said casually. ''What do you propose to do about her for a start?''

Polly forbore to make a number of acid retorts to his first remark, and instead said purposefully, ''To begin with I think she should sleep somewhere else. That room is like a mausoleum. She needs somewhere cosy and cheerful where she can't imagine that bogeys and goblins are lurking. What about the little dressing room adjoining mine?''

''Won't you need that for yourself?''

"Hardly, I'm used to being tucked away in a glorified attic, so I won't feel cooped up with a whole suite to myself," she replied dryly.

"All right. I'll tell Renata what changes you want and you can supervise them. What else?"

"Nothing at the moment. Now, if you don't mind, I'll go up and make sure that she's sleeping properly."

He rose from his chair and moved across to open the door for her. "A pity, I was hoping we could get to know each other better. However, I suppose you are still feeling pretty unkindly toward me."

"I don't feel unkindly or kindly, Mr. St. Clair," she said coolly. "You're my employer now, but Marisa is the only person in this house who will concern me."

His mouth twitched. "Can you find your way?"

"Yes, thank you. Good night."

"Good night."

All the way up the stairs she felt his eyes on her, and it was a relief to turn down the long candle-lit corridor where he could no longer see her. Marisa's room was in darkness, but as soon as she opened the door a small alarmed voice said, "Is that you, Renata?"

"No, it's me, dear. Can't you get to sleep? Where do I find your light?"

"There's a lamp on the table by the door," the voice said, sounding relieved.

Polly felt for the matches and lit the oil lamp. Fortunately she had had some experience getting such things to work. Carrying it over to the bedside, she smiled encouragingly at the child, guessing that a few minutes earlier the pig-tailed head had been buried under the bed clothes.

"Now, why aren't you asleep?" she asked gently. "Coughing?"

"I...I think there's something in the armoire," the child said with a nervous glance at the huge linen closet near by. "I heard something moving."

Polly set the lamp on the bedside table and walked to the armoire. "I expect it's a family of mice," she said cheerfully, peering inside. "There are always lots of them in old houses. I used to keep some white ones as pets when I was your age, and my brothers had guinea pigs and rabbits and a ferret called Cecil. Have you any pets?''

Marisa shook her head. ''Renata says animals make a mess.'' She hesitated, and then said in a hushed voice, ''She says there are spirits in the castle. People who died a long time ago and can't rest.''

Polly, who had yet to learn that the island was ridden with superstition and macabre folklore, decided that from now on the less Renata had to do with the child the better it would be for the little girl's peace of mind.

''And what does your uncle say?'' she asked.

''Oh, Uncle Raoul's not afraid of anything,'' Marisa told her. ''Tonio says he is as brave as a wild boar, and they are very fierce and dangerous, you know.''

''Are they? Well then, if Uncle Raoul is around I don't expect we shall come to any harm. How would you like another story to help you to get to sleep? I know—why don't you come into my room tonight, then I can be getting ready for bed while I'm telling it to you. All the beds here are so big that there's plenty of room for two, even three or four, I should think.''

''Can I? Oh, can I really?'' The child's face lit up and seeing the glow of relief, Polly knew that it would take her some time to blot out the frightening influence of old Renata's eerie tales.

An hour later, she turned down the lamp in her own room and lay back on the pillows, listening to Marisa's regular breathing close by. But as she drifted into sleep it was not the little girl's shy intelligent face that filled her thoughts, but that of a man with brilliantly blue eyes and a scarred brown cheek.

WITHIN TWO DAYS Marisa's cough had vanished and she was eating better and showing some of the high spirits normal to her age. Perhaps because of her trying time with the Vanhassons, Polly found it very easy to devote herself to her new task. Her fear that Renata would resent usurpation in one sphere of her activities was not justified. Although the old woman treated her with the reserved courtesy habitual to the islanders, there was no trace of animosity in her attitude, indeed she seemed relieved to have the child taken off her hands.

When on the third day after her arrival Polly thought Marisa was quite well enough to get up, it was arranged that they should have lunch and dinner downstairs, and during the first week Polly saw little of her employer except at mealtimes.

In the mornings she and Marisa took the elevator down to the bay and played on the beach, and in the afternoons they explored the extensive estate behind the castle. In spite of her lack of formal education, Marisa was not backward. Apparently she had learned to read very early and in the past year had devoured books far in advance of her years, with the result that she had a fund of unexpected and sometimes inappropriate knowledge and her conversation was extraordinarily grown-up.

"It's time your hair was washed. We'll do it after breakfast and then let it dry while we're down on the beach," Polly said one morning, plaiting the child's waist-length braids.

"Oh, must we? I hate it. The soap gets in my eyes and it tangles and takes so long to comb," Marisa said reluctantly.

"The soap won't get in your eyes this time, because I'll smear some cold cream around them to stop it," Polly said.

"I wish I could have it cut off like yours," Marisa said enviously.

"You can if you like. It would certainly be quicker to shampoo. But are you sure you won't miss your pigtails once they're off?"

"Oh, no! I don't like them a bit. Can I really have it cut? Now?"

"Hadn't we better ask your uncle first?"

"He won't mind. It's not his hair."

Polly smiled. "No, his hair is as short as it can be. All right, as soon as we've had breakfast we'll give you a completely new hairstyle and surprise him."

Marisa was so excited by her changed appearance that Polly feared she would be dreadfully disappointed if her uncle did not notice it at once, so shortly before lunchtime she left the child to change into a clean dress and slipped downstairs to warn him.

He was in his book-lined study leading off the hall, and when she had tapped at the door and been bidden to enter she found him lounging in a chair in well-cut riding breeches and a white shirt, a file of papers on his knees.

He rose at once and said, "This is an unexpected pleasure. What can I do for you?"

"I hope you won't be annoyed, but I've cut off Marisa's braids. A bob is much more practical and more becoming," she explained.

"I don't mind. I told you you could do as you pleased with her."

"Yes, well, that isn't really what I wanted to see you about," she said. "She's very pleased with herself—I think she's always thought herself rather an ugly duckling—and she'll expect you to notice it right away."

"And you thought I wouldn't?" he said, looking amused.

"Well. . .men often don't."

"Don't they? You seem to know a lot about us."

"I have three brothers."

"Perhaps it's because I'm not your brother that I can see you're wearing a new dress," he said, eyeing the scarlet sundress that she was intending to change for something more formal for lunch. "It's very becoming."

"Thank you. My uniforms aren't suitable for the beach. I'm going to change in a moment."

"I can't imagine why," he remarked. "That red thing suits you much better than your prison gray outfits."

Polly blushed. "I'm sorry you don't care for them, but they weren't intended to be fashionable."

"My dear child, it doesn't worry me if you want to walk around in a piece of tarpaulin," he said lazily, "or that yellow bathing suit if you like."

Her color deepened. The yellow bikini had been a present from Drew, and although she knew that her figure was reasonably presentable she had never felt completely at ease in it.

"I hope it doesn't offend the local people," she said awkwardly.

"I wouldn't think so. They're used to seeing quite a few eccentrics around Maranza. Have you been into the village, yet?"

"Not yet. We thought of going shopping tomorrow. It isn't far, is it?"

"About a mile. Tonio will run you down in the jeep."

He had no need to counterfeit approval when he saw his niece sometime later. Freed of the weight of the pigtails, Marisa's hair was less straight than it had appeared, and Polly had pinned it in a row of twirls while it was wet in order to encourage its tendency to curl. Now, with light bangs concealing the upper part of her high forehead and glossy duck's tails bobbing around her ears, she looked a different child.

During lunch she chattered vivaciously, although never interrupting either of her elders.

"Polly, are you betrothed to anyone?" she asked suddenly, eyeing a cherry that she had saved until the last.

"What put that into your head?" Polly said, smiling.

"Constancia asked me."

"Constancia should mind her own business," her uncle said from the head of the table. "Did Miss Linsey give you permission to use her first name?"

"Yes, this morning. She doesn't like being called Miss Linsey. It makes her feel old and spinsterish, doesn't it, Polly?" Marisa said sympathetically.

"How unpleasant," St. Clair said, his eyes glinting. "Perhaps I had better call you Polly, too. Are you betrothed, by the way?"

"No, I'm not," Polly said, flashing him a glance that was meant to say, *"Don't start baiting me in front of Marisa."*

"Well, I daresay there's hope, yet," he said blandly. "Don't feel too despairing."

"Do you want to get married, Polly?" Marisa asked.

"Yes, one of these days," Polly managed casually.

Marisa popped the cherry into her mouth and sucked it with relish. "Well, I hope you don't for a long time, yet," she said rather indistinctly. "We don't want you to go away, do we, Uncle Raoul?"

He folded his napkin and thrust it into a silver ring. "You shouldn't talk with your mouth full, baggage," he said. "Excuse me. I have some calls to make."

When he had left them, Marisa sipped her glass of goat's milk and looked thoughtful for a while. "Don't you like Uncle Raoul, Polly?" she asked suddenly.

"Why shouldn't I like him?" Polly said, peeling an orange.

"Sometimes you look at him in such a funny way. Your eyes go all sparkly and you stick out your chin as if you were cross with him."

Polly was saved from reply to this discomfiting observation by the entrance of Tonio with an airmail letter from England on a silver salver. Recognizing her mother's handwriting she seized it eagerly and slit open the envelope.

As he had promised, her employer had sent a cable to her parents the morning after her arrival, and Polly had written a long but slightly guarded explanation of her changed circumstances later in the day.

But the date on the first sheet of flimsy airmail paper made it clear that, at the time of writing, Mrs. Linsey could only have received the cable. The letter read:

Darling Polly,

Daddy and I were very surprised and rather worried by the cable from Mr. St. Clair that came last night. We had no idea you were unhappy with those American people. However this morning I had a visit from a most charming woman—a Mrs. Eustace who lives at Bracknell—who has known Mr. St. C. for years and assured us that you would be perfectly safe with him. Apparently he had realized that we would be worried about you and had cabled her, asking her to come over and reassure us. All the same I think you should have let us know before taking this new job. One hears of such dreadful things happening to girls abroad, and Corsica is so very far away. Do write and tell us all about it. Is it another temporary post, and what is Mr. St. C. like? I was very relieved to hear from Mrs. E. that he was half-English. I suppose I am very old-fashioned and insular, but I do feel that complete foreigners are not as reliable as English people. Do be careful with any young men you meet over there, darling. I believe Corsicans are very hot-blooded and reckless.

The rest of the letter dealt with family news with no mention of Drew being in difficulties, so Polly concluded that her money order had extricated him from his troubles without discovery.

Her employer was out to dinner that evening, so it was not until the following day when she and Marisa were climbing into the Land Rover to go to the village with Tonio that she had an opportunity to thank him for sending Mrs. Eustace to see her parents.

"Are you coming with us, Uncle Raoul?" Marisa asked hopefully as he came down the steps.

"No, I have to go over to the vineyards, *petite,*" he said. "Have you got some money to spend?"

"Yes, thank you. Polly's given me some," she said, showing him some crisp new notes that were part of Polly's first week's wage.

"That's very kind of Polly, but I think you had better give them back to her and let me finance you," he said, producing a handful of small denomination notes from his trousers pocket.

"Mr. St. Clair, I had a letter from my mother, yesterday. It was very kind of you to ask your friend to visit her and explain everything," Polly said.

He glanced at her. "Not everything, I hope, or we may have your entire family descending on us in high dudgeon," he said gravely but with laughter in his eyes.

"Carry on, Tonio." And with a casual salute he turned and walked off toward the stables.

Polly watched his tall lithe figure moving away, and then, as Tonio let in the clutch and they shot off down the drive in a flurry of gravel, she began to check her shopping list, hoping that the village would be able to supply their needs.

So far she had been too occupied with accustoming herself to the rapid sequence of events and making friends with Marisa to be more than superficially aware of Corsica as strange and fascinating country. But as they took the winding, poorly surfaced road to Maranza, she began to realize that the island and its people were not a kind of hybrid extension of France and Italy as she had previously imagined. The people they passed on the way—a grizzled old man in a black suit and black sombrero, and two women, also in black with shawls over their heads—were peasants, but they walked proudly, even with arrogance, and acknowledged the speeding jeep without servility.

Maranza proved to be a smallish place with tall color-washed, shuttered houses and a central square dominated by a church with a domed campanile. A row of black-clad old men sat on a stone bench near the doorway, chewing anise, lost in contemplation. In a pavement café shaded by a chestnut tree, younger men lounged at ease with glasses of *pastis* at their elbows. Only the women seemed busy, and Polly noticed that the alleys leading off the square were festooned with garments hung out to dry on long poles. Beyond the square was the quay, crowded with small boats, where tousle-haired boys were mending fishing nets with large wooden needles. Tonio parked the jeep near the small fruit market with its stalls piled high with pimentos, figs, cédras, maize and bananas. Then, having arranged to meet them an hour later, he went off on business of his own. Probably to join the men in the cafés, Polly thought.

The shops were few but stocked with a comprehensive variety of wares, and with Marisa to interpret for her she was able to buy all she needed. The child assured her that they could leave the packages in the back of the jeep without any fear of their being stolen and, this done, they set out to explore the narrow side streets. They were in another square, smaller than the central one, and Polly was wishing she had brought her camera so that she could snap a particularly picturesque old house with iron balconies, when a young man came out of an opening on the far side. For a second or two she did not recognize him; then, as he moved out of the shadow into the sunlight his red hair flamed, and with a cry of excitement she began to run toward him.

"Giles! Giles, wait!"

He paused on the point of walking away. At first, as he saw who it was who had called his name, he looked completely astounded. Then pleasure still mixed with incredulity lit his face.

"Good lord, it's Polly! What in the world are you doing here?" he exclaimed eagerly.

She laughed. "For a moment you looked as if you were seeing a pink elephant. I'm staying here. I left Cannes soon after you."

"You didn't say Corsica was on the itinerary. I thought you were bound for Italy," he said, taking her hands.

"So I was, but I'm not with the Vanhassons anymore. As a matter of fact, Mrs. Vanhasson sacked me the day you left."

"Sacked you!" he repeated in astonishment. "Whatever for?"

Polly colored. "Mr. Vanhasson had a roving eye, and she thought I was encouraging him."

"Great snakes, what a rotten thing to happen!" Giles said indignantly. "I wish I'd known he was making passes at you. I'd have soon sorted him out, the swine! But how did you end up here? Surely you haven't been home in the meantime?"

She hesitated, instinct warning her that it might be unwise to give too detailed an account of her arrival on the island. "No, I was very lucky. The day after I got thrown out, I met someone who needed a nanny rather urgently. But what are you doing here?''

He smiled. ''Well, I *was* just passing through, but I think I may stop over for a while now. Look, we can't talk properly here. Let's find a café and a couple of cooling drinks.''

''All right, if you can run to three. I've got my charge with me,'' Polly said, looking around for Marisa, who was absorbed in petting a kitten and had not yet noticed that Polly had met a friend. Although reluctant to leave the kitten, she answered Polly's call with her usual ready obedience and responded to Giles's ''Hello'' with a shy curtsey.

''Polly, do you think I could have a kitten now that you're here? I would so like one,'' she said, as they went in search of a café.

''We'll ask Uncle Raoul at lunchtime,'' Polly said.

''Who's Uncle Raoul?'' Giles asked.

''My employer and Marisa's guardian,'' she explained, wondering what he would say when he discovered that Uncle Raoul was also the man he had described as ''one hell of a lady-killer.'' Pleased as she was by Giles's unexpected advent she foresaw complications.

''What's happened to your friends?'' she asked, when they were settled in a café and he had ordered three glasses of fresh lemon juice.

''Oh, we parted company at Rapallo. I felt like being on my own for a while and decided to have a look around this place. Pretty dead-end, isn't it? Even the larger towns are half-asleep.''

''The scenery is superb,'' Polly said.

''Yes, top class—but man cannot live by scenery alone,'' he replied with a look that she found faintly disturbing. ''Meeting again like this—well, it makes me think there's something in fate, after all.''

She smiled. ''It's a lovely surprise. I've been wondering how you were getting along.''

''Have you? Have you really, Polly?'' His hand moved across the table toward hers, and then, with a glance at Marisa, he withdrew it and lit a cigarette, rather red around the ears. "Look, d'you have any more free time here?" he asked presently. "I mean, can I see you tonight? I don't suppose there's much in the way of entertainment but we could have a couple of drinks and trot around the harbor."

"That would be lovely," Polly said. "I haven't been out at night, yet, but I'm quite free if I want to."

"Where do I collect you?"

"Oh—I think it would be better if I met you, Giles. Where are you staying?"

"I spent last night in a room over one of the cafés—not exactly a five-star joint, but at least there were no bugs around. I would think the people who own it will put me up for another night or two. It's the main square, a place called Romanetti's," he said. "But why can't I pick you up?"

"I'm not quite sure what time I'll be ready. Oh dear...."

She broke off, remembering that it was at least a mile from the castle gates to the outskirts of the village and about a quarter of that distance from the gates to the castle. The prospect of walking so far in the dark was not alluring.

"Perhaps you had better collect me after all," she said. "But I'm afraid it's rather a long way."

"That doesn't matter. The son of the chap who owns the café has a motorbike that I daresay he'll rent out to me if I make it worth his while. Where exactly are you?"

"It's called Castel Maranza, an estate about a—"

"Great Scott, you don't mean you're at that Hollywood setup just along the coast, do you?" he cut in.

"Yes, that's right. I suppose you can see it from the quay. I hadn't noticed," she said.

"Too true you can see it! I say, you have fallen on your feet. What's it like inside? Full of scurrying minions and gold plate?"

"Not exactly, but it is rather opulent," Polly admitted.

Giles made an impressed face. "Uncle Raoul must be

one of the robber barons," he remarked. "Has he got any nephews who could do with a holiday tutor?"

"No, I'm afraid not," Polly said, laughing. "But he might let me ask you to tea if you'd like to see it at close quarters."

"Tea! I would expect champagne in diamond-studded goblets," Giles said. "What time shall I sneak up to the tradesman's entrance?"

"Around eightish should be all right," Polly said. Then, glancing at her watch, "Oh, heavens, poor Tonio will be waiting for us. We must run, Marisa, or he'll think we're lost. Goodbye, Giles. Thanks for the lemonade. See you later." And, seizing Marisa's hand, she hurried her away with a backward smile and wave before they turned the corner.

Raoul was a few minutes late for lunch that day and after apologizing for keeping them waiting he said, "Did you get all you wanted?"

Polly said that they had, and Marisa added excitedly, "Polly is going to make me some shorts for playing on the beach, Uncle Raoul."

"That's very kind of her," he said. "Is sewing an accepted part of your duties, Polly?"

"Oh, yes, it's quite usual," she said, with a smile. "Marisa's clothes are all beautifully made, but they're a little old-fashioned, and I think she needs something lighter and more casual for playing in." Then she said, "Mr. St. Clair, I met a friend in the village this morning. Do you mind if I go out this evening for a little while?"

"Of course not, you are free to come and go as you please," he answered. "Why not ask your friend to dinner? You'll find the cafés rather rough and ready. But perhaps you would rather be alone."

"Actually I'd planned to dine here as usual and go out afterwards," she said.

"Oh well, in that case just tell Tonio what time you want the car. He's always glad of an excuse to spend an evening cardsharping."

"Thank you, but my friend is picking me up. I won't need to bother Tonio."

He regarded her keenly for a moment and then said,
"I see. I hope your friend is a good driver. Our roads
can be tricky to a stranger."

And, for the time being, that was the close of the subject.

While Marisa was sleeping through the early afternoon heat, Polly unwrapped the parcel of material that
they had brought in the village and set about cutting it
out. She became so engrossed in her task that she did
not hear a light rap on the door, and the tune she was
humming to herself ended on an indrawn breath when
she caught sight of Raoul watching her from the doorway.

"I did knock," he said. "May I come in for a moment?"

She nodded, indicating that Marisa was dozing in the
next room. "I'm just cutting out her shorts," she said
softly. "It's rather complicated without a paper pattern."

He strolled across to the window and sat down on the
oak settle.

"I believe there's an old sewing machine somewhere
around that might be some help. I'll tell Renata to hunt
it out and get it oiled," he said.

"Is there? It would be a tremendous help. I don't
mind sewing by hand, but it takes much longer."

"Did you make that dress you are wearing?"

She glanced down at her white cotton dress patterned
with cornflowers.

"Yes, I make most of my things," she said, wondering what he wanted. He had not come to her room for a
casual chat about dressmaking, of that she was certain.

"I'm afraid the shops in the village are not up to
much," he said. "I shall be driving over to Ajaccio later
in the week if you'd care to come."

"Will I be able to get a zipper there, do you think?"

His mouth curved. "Ajaccio is the capital of Corsica," he said dryly. "It doesn't compare with London
or Paris, but I think it's sufficiently civilized to provide
zippers."

Polly bit her lip. "I'm afraid you must think me very ignorant," she said uncomfortably.

"Not at all, most foreigners know little or nothing about Corsica, except that Napoleon was born here and that the natives are reputed to be hot-tempered and handy with knives," he said mildly.

"Oh, that reminds me...." Polly went to the dressing table and opened the drawer in which she had put the knife that he had given her on board the *Corsair*. Flushing at the memory of the incident, she handed it to him.

"Are you sure you might not need it again?" he asked quizzically.

Her colour deepened, and hurriedly turning back to the table where she had been cutting out, she said, "What is the writing on the blade?"

"It's an inscriptions that's incised on all knives of this type. It means 'May my wound be deadly.'"

"What a bloodthirsty motto!"

"Naturally, this is a vendetta knife," he said casually.

Polly straightened, her eyes widening. "You mean... people have been killed with it?"

"Of course, did you think it was an ornament?"

"I certainly wouldn't have kept it all this time if I'd known it had been...used," she said with a shiver. "Why, it's a murder weapon!"

"We don't regard vendetta killings as murder," he said calmly. "They are punishments for wrongs."

She stared at him. "But your father was English. You can't possibly appprove of that sort of thing," she protested.

He ran his thumb over the razor-sharp blade. "In England certain crimes are punishable by the state, but others, equally serious, are not. For instance, an Englishman can take another man's wife or seduce a young girl."

He paused, watching her with that penetrating gaze that she found so disconcerting. "Both those things can, and often do, go unpunished. Here people don't wait for the law. That's why in Corsica women don't have to worry about walking home after dark or passing through lonely places. You could hike from Bastia to Calvi without any fear of being molested.''

''Do you really mean that if someone ran off with your wife or seduced your sister, you would kill him?'' she asked, appalled.

He shrugged. ''As you say, I'm half-English, so perhaps I wouldn't actually kill him. But I'd certainly make sure that he didn't try it twice,'' he said with a steely glint in his eyes.

''But . . . but it's so uncivilized!'' she exclaimed. ''And anyway, your wife might be really in love with him—people can't help that happening—and your sister might be just as much to blame as the man.''

''Quite possibly, but in Corsica men don't stand by and allow their women to make fools of themselves,'' he said sternly.

''Don't the women have *any* say in the matter?'' she asked with sarcasm.

He did not reply, and for some minutes there was a strained silence. Then, as calmly as if they had been discussing the weather, he said, ''It must have been a pleasant surprise for you—meeting your friend today. We don't get many tourists as a rule.''

''Yes, it was a lovely surprise.''

''A man or a woman?''

''A man.''

''Have you known him long?''

''Not very long. I met him at Cannes.''

''A friend of your American family?''

Polly fidgeted with the tape measure. Why should he be so interested?

''No. We met on the beach. He used to watch the children while I had a swim.''

''You mean he picked you up?'' he asked, with raised eyebrows.

Her color rose again. ''I suppose you could call it that. We weren't formally introduced by a mutual friend.''

"Do you think it's wise to make friends with someone whose background you don't know?"

Polly's eyes flashed. "You're hardly in a position to criticize me on that score, Mr. St. Clair," she said frigidly. "Giles Barrington has never forced me to go anywhere against my will, and I would think he'd be horrified if he knew how I came to be here."

He grinned at her. "I suspect that you have a nasty temper when you're roused. Are you going to tell him how you came here?"

"Probably." She paused and then added acidly, "You needn't worry. As he isn't a Corsican he won't plunge a knife into you."

"But then I haven't deserved it, have I?" he said mockingly.

A rush of vivid color stained her face, but she forced herself to hold his glance. "I would think that frightening me half out of my wits would be quite sufficient justification," she retorted.

"Oh, come now, you weren't really so terrified, and if you'd known a little more about Corsicans you'd have had no qualms at all," he said carelessly. "We never force our attentions on unwilling women, particularly Englishwomen who are notoriously cold and reserved."

"That's a very sweeping generalization," Polly said scornfully. "How do you know what Englishwomen are like?"

"I've met quite a few."

"Perhaps you were unlucky. You can't expect to dazzle everyone," she countered with deadly sweetness.

He laughed. "You're a formidable adversary when you forget to be prim. Why does it annoy you so much that I find most Englishwomen insipid?"

"It doesn't annoy me at all. I just think it's a mistake to put that sort of label on any race of people."

"But you're inclined to think that Corsicans are pretty callous and savage."

"Not at all," she said gently. "I'm reserving judgment until I know more of them. I don't expect that you are typical, Mr. St. Clair."

The barb was wasted for as usual he only laughed.

"I must be off," he said, rising. "By the way, could you bring yourself to use my Christian name or is it against regulations? Being called Mr. St. Clair doesn't make me feel old and bachelorish, but it might ease our relations if you were a little less formal."

"It's not usual to call one's employer by a first name," she said.

"But then this has never been a usual arrangement, has it?" he said dryly. "Do you object to my calling you Polly?"

"That's rather different."

"Is it? I fail to see why. However, we have to argue it out later. I have an appointment."

Polly did not see him again that day as he was out to dinner, and when she returned to the castle after a pleasant evening with Giles, the rest of the household appeared to have gone to bed. But as she undressed and brushed her hair, she remembered his derisive remark about Englishwomen being too insipid for his taste, and wondered why it rankled.

CHAPTER FOUR

THE FOLLOWING MORNING Polly, who had not slept very well, was roused by a gentle pressure on her shoulder. Opening her eyes she found Constancia standing by the bed with a note in her hand. Blinking away her drowsiness she unfolded it and read: "I shall have to go to Ajaccio today. Can you and Marisa be ready in an hour? R."

Her bag was on the bedside cabinet and after finding a pencil, Polly wrote "Yes" on the bottom of the note, gave it back to Constancia and then swallowed a quick cup of tea before scrambling out of bed to wake the child. Their breakfast of cornflakes, freshly baked *brioches* and fruit was ready for them in a small room along the corridor when they had dressed, and it was a few minutes before half-past seven when they went downstairs to find Raoul smoking a cigarette in the hall. He was wearing an immaculate suit of light-weight gray cloth, a white silk shirt and dark tie, and Polly was glad she had put on a slim-skirted dress of beige and white silk with a matching jacket instead of an ordinary cotton dress.

"Sorry to cut your beauty sleep, but it's better to make the trip before the sun is high," he said, bending to let Marisa press her good-morning kiss on his cheek.

Outside Tonio was giving a final polish to the hood of the cream Jaguar that had presumably been brought over from Cannes by a car ferry. *Unless he keeps duplicate cars on either side of the water,* Polly thought with a smile to herself.

She intended to get into the back with Marisa, but opening the forward passenger door Raoul said, "Come in front. You'll enjoy a better view."

"Enjoy yourself last night?" he asked, as they set off.

"Yes, thank you."

"How long is Barrington staying here?"

"I'm not sure. I think he's hoping to do some rock climbing, and this seems like quite a good center for it."

"Yes, it is—if he knows his stuff and has the right gear. Incidentally, Tonio is taking a note down later to ask him to dine with us tonight. We'll be back before seven and I dare say he'd like to see as much of you as possible."

Polly wondered if there was an edge to his tone, but she said quietly. "Thank you. I know he's very interested in the castle and would like to see the inside of it."

"I gather he's the boy you were with that morning outside the hotel."

"Yes, that's right. Although he's not exactly a boy. He's twenty-four."

He glanced at her with a tilted eyebrow and she wished she had held her tongue.

The fifty-mile drive to the capital took them through mountainous countryside of such barbaric beauty that Polly spent most of the journey leaning forward and trying to photograph each new panorama on her mind's eye. The sloping olive groves bordered by grotesquely shaped cacti, the high passes through dim green forest and the jagged boulder-strewn ravines made her long to be able to paint. In places the road was so bad that even the superbly sprung Jaguar bounced and jolted over the rutted surface, and more than once the outside wheels were only a few feet from the edge of a precipitous drop into a deep gorge. But although her brother Drew had often terrified her by the way he roared around English byways in his ramshackle M.G., she was not nervous.

Raoul spent most of the drive talking to Marisa and his lean brown fingers rested lightly on the steering wheel, but it was evident that he had complete mastery of the powerful car and that he knew every sharp descent and blind bend on the road. At one point, halfway up an immense granite cliff, they met a dilapidated mail bus, the roof rack piled high with a heterogeneous collection of baggage, the interior crowded with a motley assortment of passengers. It seemed impossible for the two vehicles to be able to pass each other, but the driver pulled in close to the cliff face and Raoul inched the Jaguar past it with less than a foot to spare.

"I wouldn't care to drive along here at night," Polly said, when the bus had been safely negotiated.

"No, I'm afraid our roads aren't too good, but it does spare us from an influx of sightseers," he said. "Do you drive?"

She shook her head. "No, my father's car is nearly always in use, and proper lessons are rather expensive."

"I'll teach you if you like," he said. "It's useful to be able to hop into a car in a hurry."

"Oh, but aren't you much too busy?" she said.

"I have an hour to spare now and then, and if you can drive in Corsica you can drive anywhere."

"Antonetta cried when you taught her to drive," Marisa said over his shoulder. "She said you swore at her."

He grinned. "Very probably. Every time we met an obstacle or a sharp bend she flung up her hands and expected the car to drive itself." Then he said to Polly, "Antonetta is the daughter of a friend of mine. She's at school in Paris, but she'll be home in a few days. I think you'll like her." He broke off to hoot at a goat that was ambling along the center of the road, and then went on, "She probably won't recommend me as an instructor. Our lessons generally ended in hysterics."

"Oh, dear, that isn't very encouraging," Polly said. "I shall probably fling up my hands, too."

"I doubt it. "You've got more sense than she has and you obviously don't panic in a crisis."

Polly turned her head away and pretended to be gazing at a group of eucalyptus trees. Was he referring to the events on the *Corsair*?

"By the way, have you heard from your brother, yet?" he asked.

"No, I expect I'll have to wait until I get home to find

out what it was all about,'' she said. ''Drew loathes writing letters, even postcards.''

''Does he always expect you to get him out of his fixes?''

''Yes, I suppose he does. We're twins, you see, and although the other boys are dears, we've always felt like a pair. He's helped me out of scrapes, too. It isn't a one-way arrangement.''

''I wish I had a brother,'' Marisa said with a long-drawn sigh. She had not yet asked her uncle about having a kitten and guessing what was on her mind, Polly said, ''Mr. St. Clair, there's a family of kittens in the village. D'you think Marisa could have one as a pet? We'd train it to be clean and they don't eat much.''

''I don't see why not,'' he replied. ''It will mean that in five years' time we shall be overrun with them, I dare say, but we can deal with that when the time comes. Don't throttle me, baggage. You'll have us all in the ditch.'' This he said as Marisa flung her arms around his neck and bestowed a joyful and smacking kiss on his ear. ''You're getting very demonstrative these days. It must be Polly's influence. She'd better teach you that there's a time and place for everything. Choking the man at the wheel can be dangerous.''

Marisa, sensing that he was teasing her, giggled happily. After a minute she said, ''What does 'monstrative mean?''

Raoul looked at Polly. ''You're her mentor,'' he said.

''It means showing how one feels about a person. You thought it was nice of Uncle Raoul to say you could have the kitten, so you demonstrated that you thought him kind by kissing him. See?''

Marisa nodded, mouthing the word to herself. She loved long words and often made Polly burst out laughing at malapropisms. But she did not laugh when, with the embarrassing logic of an eight-year-old, Marisa said thoughtfully, ''It was kind of Uncle Raoul to promise to teach you to drive, wasn't it?''

Polly quelled an impulse to tell her charge that little girls should be seen and not heard and said, as coolly as she could manage, "Well, yes...but that's rather different." Too late, she realized that the reply to this was inevitably. "Why?"

"Because you are related to Uncle Raoul and I'm not."

"Tonio isn't related to Constancia, but he kisses her all the time," Marisa said reasonably.

"I expect they're betrothed or something," Polly said.

"If they aren't they soon will be, or you may find yourself in the middle of one of those feuds that you disapprove of so much," Raoul said dryly. "Constancia's father is a real old diehard and Tonio will find himself at the wrong end of a shotgun if he thinks he can amuse himself in that direction."

They arrived in Ajaccio shortly before ten, and Raoul parked the car in the Place de Gaulle and arranged to meet them at half-past twelve when he had completed his business.

Polly was anxious to see as much as she could of the city but she did not want to overtire Marisa, so, after they had strolled along the lime-shaded Cours Grandval and had ice creams and cold drinks in a café, she suggested that they should take a ride in one of the horse-drawn victorias that were plying for rent. Raoul was already there when they returned to the car a few minutes late because they had stopped to look in some shop windows.

"Find your zipper?" he asked, as they hurried up, breathless and a little weary from moving among the crowds that thronged the main streets.

Polly nodded, glad to be relieved of the armful of packages she had acquired.

"One can't miss the fact that Napoleon was born here, can one?" she said, watching him stow them safely in the trunk. "I've never seen so many statues of one person."

"Wait till you see the Ink Pot, or have you already feasted your eyes?" he asked.

"The Ink Pot?"

He grinned. "A particularly hideous memorial in the Place du Diamant with the old boy sitting on a horse and his four brothers striking attitudes on the corners."

She laughed. "Oh no, we must have missed that one, what a shame."

He reached for the last of her parcels and in taking it his fingers brushed hers. What happened in that fraction of a second, that tiny fragment of time before the parcel left her hands and was put away, was something outside her experience, something strange and oddly frightening. Later, during lunch at an imposing hotel that reminded her of Cannes, she decided that it had been either her imagination or else the result of the heat and a longer than usual interval between meals.

There was certainly no other sensible explanation for her heart seeming to have stopped short for a beat and for her throat constricting.

HAVING GROWN UP in a predominantly masculine household with her brothers' friends outnumbering her own, Polly had never viewed the opposite sex as a mysterious species whose thoughts and emotions were totally different from those of women. So she had never understood why some girls began to flutter and giggle and adopt all kinds of artificial airs and, graces as soon as a presentable man came within a few yards of them. And when her friends confided to her that a certain man made them feel weak at the knees just by looking at them, or interpreted some perfectly normal gesture or remark as a secret signal of smoldering passion, she was by turns amused at their absurdity or puzzled by her own failure to share their transports. None of the men she had known since her first date when she was seventeen had caused her the breathless excitement that her girl friends experienced regularly, and even Giles, whom she liked better than any of them, did not send shivers down her spine when he smiled at her or touched her. So the possibility that a man with whom she was still very much on her guard could, by the most fleeting of accidental contacts, produce one of the sensations from which she had always seemed to be immune was so ridiculous that consciously she did not even admit it was a possibility. If asked, she would have admitted that Raoul St. Clair was a man whom some girls would find attractive, even fascinating. But even discounting the circumstances that surrounded their association he was not, she told herself firmly, the type of man she could ever wholeheartedly admire and respect.

He was too autocratic, too self-sufficient, too bold.

After lunch he took them to see the museum and the chapel containing the Bonaparte family tombs in the Fesch Palace. When they emerged the city was still wrapped in noonday somnolence. Every bench in the tropical gardens were occupied by sleeping figures and the shops were either closed or unattended. Even the gendarmes had disappeared.

"It's too hot to do any more sightseeing today. We'll go back to the hotel and rest for an hour before leaving," Raoul said.

They had the fan-cooled terrace at the back of the hotel to themselves and, with her glass of orange juice in her hand, Marisa suddenly dropped off to sleep. Freeing the glass from her hot little fingers, Polly set it on the painted cane table and leaned back to sip her own Dubonnet *cassis,* a refreshing long drink made from the wine, a shot of blackcurrant juice and soda water. She had already taken off her jacket and presently Raoul followed suit, rolling up the sleeves of his shirt and crossing his long legs.

"Where are your sunglasses?" he asked suddenly.

"I forgot to bring them."

He reached into an inside pocket of his jacket, removed a gray leather case and tossed it onto her lap. "Put those on."

"What about you?"

"I don't have to worry about wrinkles."

She put the glasses on. They were the expensive minutely tinted kind and effectively shielded her eyes from the dazzling glare.

"Go to sleep if you want to," he said.

Polly closed her eyes but she could never sleep in the daytime and presently she opened them again. Raoul was smoking and looking at the garden. He was sitting with the scarred side of his face toward her and, not for the first time, she wondered how he had come by it and what he had looked like when his cheek was unmarked and before maturity had stamped his strongly cut features. Every line of his face suggested pride and dominance and a hard unyielding will, she thought, everything but his mouth, which should have been thin-lipped and harsh and, instead, was oddly gentle with the rather full lower lip that was said to indicate tenderness and warmth.

She was looking at the scar again when he turned and caught her eye. His brows arched derisively and his teeth showed white against the dark bronze of his skin.

"Why not ask if you're curious?" he said softly.

Polly crimsoned. "I'm sorry. I didn't mean to stare."

"I don't mind." He dropped the end of his cigarette into a stone ashtray where it sizzled momentarily before the water inside extinguished it. "Do disfigurements have a horrid fascination for you?"

"No, of course not," she said quickly. "Anyway, that isn't a disfigurement. It gives you rather a...a dashing, piratical look."

He grinned. "From you, that's a handsome compliment."

She hesitated, remembering their conversation the previous afternoon. "It's not a vendetta scar, is it?" she asked.

He regarded her gravely. "I didn't get it falling down the stairs."

"You mean...you fought somebody?"

"Two of them, as a matter of fact."

"B-but what happened?"

He shrugged. "My knife was longer and sharper than theirs. It wasn't pleasant, but these things happen from time to time."

The solemnity of his tone gave him away. Polly stared at him, saw the gleam in his eyes and with an unwilling smile said, "Oh, what nonsense. I don't believe a word of it."

His lips twitched. "Poor Polly, how we do torment you," he said lazily.

"How did you get that scar—truthfully?" she asked.

"In England, as a matter of fact. I was at school in Rutland for a year or two and I spent one Christmas holiday at the home of a lad I was friendly with. We had fencing lessons at school and when we found a couple of old rapiers in a boxroom we thought we'd practice dueling. Being a couple of young fools we didn't bother about fixing up some kind of mask or buttoning the blades. Tom had a stronger wrist than I had, so the result was that I spent the rest of the holiday in bed."

"Oh, what a horrible thing to happen! The other boy and his parents must have felt dreadfully bad about it," Polly said.

"Yes, they were much more upset than I was. Poor old Tom couldn't sit down for a week after his father had finished with him, so he really came off worst. On the whole it was a pretty useful accident. It taught both of us not to take chances."

"I expect you would have learned that eventually by some less drastic means," Polly said soberly.

His glance grew teasing again. "It's had its advantages. Women don't seem to mind it. It stirs their maternal instincts."

"Anyone less likely to make women feel maternal I can't imagine," Polly said unthinkingly.

"That's frank of you. Why not?"

She wished the lenses of his glasses were darker so that she would be screened from his uncomfortably keen regard.

"One feels maternal about people who are helpless and unsure of themselves," she said awkwardly.

"That proves how little you know about your own sex," he remarked sardonically. "If women are maternally minded they can long to mother a gorilla."

"Well, I'm obviously not one of them, so I wouldn't

know," she said coolly. "The only people I ever want to fuss over are children."

"No, you're one of the victims of emancipation," he said casually. "By instinct you're the type who wants a man to track you down and grab you by the hair, but your education tells you that anything he can do you can do just as well. The result is that when the primitive side of you wants to give in and take whatever's coming, the New Woman element urges you to fight back."

Polly gave him what she hoped was a nonchalant smile. "You ought to set up as a psychoanalyst, Mr. St. Clair. You'd make a fortune," she said.

"I probably would at that. The workings of the female mind aren't as complicated as they seem once one grasps the basic trends. For instance, you think that by calling me Mr. St. Clair you can keep a check on my 'insufferable' behavior, don't you?"

She sipped her drink for a moment before replying, and then, stirring the pale mauve froth with the straw, said, "Not at all—Raoul. I was merely being polite, but if you really don't mind your employees using your Christian name, it's all one to me. And of course I've discovered by now that you don't mean to be insufferable. You're just a bit eccentric."

He laughed at her. "A brave stand, but you may regret it once we're back in the wilderness." Then, sliding his chair closer, he reached out an arm and took her hand. "Why not call a truce? You're not still angry with me for shanghaiing you, are you?"

"No, I suppose not—though I ought to be," she said slowly.

"Oh, forget what you ought to be. Life is too short for bothering with what's over and done with."

"All right, then, we'll call a truce," she agreed.

"Good girl!" He glanced at his watch. "It's time we were moving. Wake the infant up, will you? I'm going for a wash."

He was still holding her hand, and before he stood up he lifted it from the arm of her chair. For a moment she felt the warmth of lips against her knuckles and then, picking up his jacket, he turned and went into the hotel.

AS SHE SAT at the dressing table and buffed her nails later that evening, Polly wondered how Giles would react when he discovered the identity of her employer in about half an hour's time. Marisa was already in bed, having fallen asleep again on the drive home. Now, as Polly looked through the open communicating door, she could see the child's head half buried in the pillow.

I expect she's dreaming about the kitten she's going to choose tomorrow, she thought with a smile. Already she was fonder of the little Corsican than of any of her previous charges, and the satisfaction of seeing how rapidly the child was blossoming under more lenient and understanding supervision more than compensated for her worries over the Vanhassons.

As she smoothed pale pink cream into the backs of her hands, she could not help thinking of the incident on the hotel terrace in Ajaccio. She was thankful Raoul had not paused to see her cheeks flame before disappearing into the hotel. He would almost certainly have commented on her reaction, and probably their truce would have ended before it had begun.

She sighed, wishing she did not blush so easily—especially at commonplaces. For that, outside England, was all the gesture was. Latin men bowed over women's hands and kissed the fingertips instead of crushing the bones in a hearty vise as Englishmen did. One did not redden like a lobster over a British handshake, so why do it at the equivalent gesture abroad?

It was not, she thought vexedly, as if it was the first time it had happened to her. Two years ago her eldest brother, Nicholas, had brought an Austrian friend home for a few days, and on being introduced to Mrs. Linsey and her daughter, Stefan had clicked his heels together and kissed their hands with a gallantry they had both thought delightful. In fact, it had become a joke between them and he had done it every morning and evening of his stay, amused by their enjoyment of the custom. So why had Raoul's method of sealing their peace treaty sent color coursing to the roots of her hair like any gauche teenager?

The answer, of course, was that he had a flair for throwing her off balance merely by using a certain inflexion or raising an ironic eyebrow. She would just have to learn to steel herself against reacting noticeably.

Adding a string of coffee-tinted pearls to the scooped neckline of her dress, which fortunately was crease resistant and had survived the day's drive without becoming jaded, Polly clipped small matching studs to her ears, blotted her lipstick, took a final peep at Marisa and went downstairs.

Raoul was waiting for her in the yellow salon and had just asked her what she wanted to drink when they heard Tonio and Giles in the hall. A moment later the steward-cum-butler appeared in the doorway to announce their guest.

As soon as she saw Giles's jaw drop, Polly knew that she should have forewarned him. As it was, she could only send up a silent prayer he would have sufficient *savoir faire* to contain his secondary reactions until later.

"Good evening. Welcome to Castel Maranza," Raoul said courteously. "Polly and I are having a Cap Corse. Will you join us or would you prefer something stronger?"

For a minute Polly thought that Giles was going to turn on his heel and walk out, but then, with a glance at her that made her feel doubly guilty, he recovered himself and said in a carefully controlled voice. "Good evening, sir. It's very good of you to ask me up. I'll join you if I may."

"Polly tells me that you're keen on rock climbing," Raoul said, moving past her to reach the trolley on which the drinks were arranged. As he did so he looked at her, and although his face was impassive she knew by the glitter of his eyes that in spite of Giles's quick recovery he had a very fair idea of the situation.

With Polly putting one or two questions that she hoped were not too fatuous, the two men discussed rock

climbing and mountaineering until Raoul suggested that
they should adjourn to the dinner table. As he had done
with her, Raoul set himself to put the younger man at
ease, but this time his efforts were less successful. Giles
listened to his remarks with an attention that was almost
too deferential, and took his share of the conversation,
but Polly sensed that he was very far from relaxed.

While they were having coffee Tonio came in and
spoke to his master in an undertone.

"I'm afraid I shall have to leave you for half an
hour," he said. "Two of my workers are fighting. I'd
better try to straighten the matter out. Help yourself to
drinks, Barrington, and look after Polly, will you?"

He had barely had time to close the door behind him
before Giles turned on her, his jaw taut.

"Just what is all this?" he demanded angrily. "Why
didn't you tell me that fellow owned this place, and
what the devil are you doing working for him after what
I told you in Cannes?"

Polly drew in a breath, her fingers locked in her lap.
"I'm sorry, Giles. Truly I am. I meant to tell you, but I
thought you might be put out so I let it wait for a while.
I didn't know until we were in the car this morning that
he'd asked you up here tonight."

"Put out!" he exploded. "I'll say I'm put out! A fine
ass you've made out of me. Well, I hope it gave you a
kick."

He swung away, his hands thrust into his trouser
pockets, his underlip jutting. He looked so much like a
cross little boy that Polly had to suppress the quiver of a
smile, but, genuinely contrite she jumped up and laid
a penitent hand on his arm.

"Oh, Giles dear, you must know it wasn't deliberate
and that I didn't find it a scrap funny," she said pleading-
ly. "It was stupid of me not to have explained the whole
thing to you at once. Please don't be so angry with me."

For a few seconds he continued to scowl at the carpet
and then he looked at her hand on his sleeve and his expression lightened a little.

"Suppose you explain now," he said gruffly.

Under the circumstances Polly knew it would be fatal to reveal the whole story so, as briefly as she could, she gave him an abridged version, explaining how Raoul had rescued her from the gambling club and offered her a post as nurse-cum-governess to his ward.

He heard her out in silence, but as soon as she had finished, he exclaimed. "But, great snakes, you might have found yourself in an even worse mess. How could you possibly know his offer was genuine?"

She bit her lip. "I suppose it was rather risky, but somehow, in spite of what you'd said about him, I . . . I thought he seemed safe."

He clapped a hand to his forehead and let out an exasperated breath. "Ye gods! Everyone knows the Riviera is swarming with confidence tricksters and worse! You must have been off your head, Polly!"

"Well, it's all turned out well, and I'll never do it again, I promise."

"I should damn well hope not," he said severely. "If you want my advice—which doesn't seem to have carried much weight so far, I must say—you'll pack your gear and get out as fast as you can. A man with his reputation isn't fit to employ someone like you."

"Oh, Giles, that's not fair. The things you heard about were probably tremendously exaggerated, and I can't leave Marisa to that grim old woman again. She was frightening the poor little scrap out of her wits with tales of hobgoblins and spirits."

"Make him get someone else, then," Giles retorted grimly. "He can afford to pay a whole corps of nurses."

"But I'm beginning to like it here," she said. "You wouldn't object if you hadn't heard all that tittle-tattle."

"There's no smoke without a fire," he said stubbornly. "One has only to look at the fellow to see what type he is."

"But if he was really such a bad character he wouldn't have bothered to get me out of that awful club," Polly argued.

"He might have done—for his own ends. Anyway, no decent man would have brought you over here by boat with no other women on board. If that got around, your reputation would have had it.''

"How can it get around? You're the only person who knows apart from my parents. And he did send a friend of his to see them, remember. That was a thoughtful thing to do.''

"I still don't like it," Giles persisted obstinately. "He's not English, and foreigners can be darned tricky.''

"His father was English and he was educated in England," Polly said.

"That makes it worse," Giles said crossly. "People with mixed blood are always a bit off the mark.''

Polly stiffened. "That's a horrible thing to say," she said coldly. "Practically everyone has mixed blood of some kind. What possible difference does it make?''

"All the difference," he told her sharply. "Half-breeds have the worst characteristics of both races. It's a known fact.''

"No, it isn't—it's just a silly old wives' tale that people go on repeating because they can't be bothered to find out the truth," Polly flared. "Any minute now you'll start insulting all foreigners!''

She moved away from him, her chin thrust out, her eyes bright with indignation.

Giles struggled with his deeply rooted convictions and his feelings for her.

"Look, don't be mad at me," he said presently. "Actually I don't give a damn how mixed people are. It's just that I'm worried about you staying here. Don't let's fight, Polly.''

She wavered, not wanting quarrel with him and yet still provoked by the views he had expressed—provoked and oddly disappointed in him. After a moment or two her tension slackened and she managed a pale smile.

"I'm sorry. I shouldn't have flown off the handle like that. No—'' as he opened his mouth to speak ''—let's forget the whole thing.''

Giles studied her anxiously for a moment and then he lifted his shoulders, sighed, and said, "Okay, but there's one thing I must say—and don't get into a paddy again because I'm not saying it *will* happen." He paused, moved closer and laid his hands on her shoulders. "If—only if, mind you—St. Clair should get out of line while I'm around, you will tell me?"

Polly hesitated and then she laughed and said dryly, "All right, I'll tell you. But you needn't worry, Giles, I'm just a robot in nurse's uniform as far as he's concerned. He's agreeable to me out of habit, but he told me yesterday that Englishwomen are much too insipid to appeal to him."

Giles made a face. "Did he indeed? That was candid of him—though not particularly civil, I would have thought. If you ask me, he'd be lucky to have a chance to lick your boots." He smiled at her. "Sure you've forgiven me?"

She nodded. "It was all my fault for not confiding in you sooner."

His hands tightened on her shoulders and for a moment she thought he was going to kiss her, but almost immediately he let her go and said, "How about a drink to soothe our jangled nerves?"

When, in rather more than an hour, Raoul returned, they were sitting side by side on one of the couches, their fingers loosely interlocked, laughing together at a story Giles had just told.

As soon as Raoul entered Giles released her hand and stood up, and Polly could not help wishing that, in doing so he had not made it appear that they had passed her employer's absence in a more intimate fashion than was actually the case.

"Was the trouble serious?" she asked.

Raoul shook his head. "No, nothing out of the way. Just the result of too much wine. It's all over now." He turned to Giles. "I was wondering if you would care to come over for a swim tomorrow, Barrington. Polly and Marisa generally spend the morning down in the cove and I shall be out for lunch, so perhaps you'd like to keep them company."

"Thank you very much, sir. I'd be delighted," Giles said with alacrity. "Well, you've had a long day so I'll be pushing off. Thank you for an excellent dinner. Good night, Polly. See you tomorrow.''

Raoul rang the bell for Tonio and then escorted him out, leaving Polly to reflect that the evening had not been as catastrophic as she had feared. When Raoul returned she was prepared to thank him for having Giles to dinner and then to say good night, but he accepted her thanks with a smile and then said, ''Don't run away for a moment—or are you exhausted?''

''No, not particularly. Was there something you wanted to say about Marisa?''

''Not that I can think of. You're making an even better job of cheering her up than I had anticipated,'' he said. Then he asked, ''Did I detect a certain undercurrent of strain earlier on?''

Polly fidgeted with her necklace. ''Giles didn't realize who I was working for,'' she said, a good deal embarrassed. ''That is, he didn't know he'd met you before.''

''And for reasons that I don't find hard to deduce, he doesn't approve of the setup, I imagine.''

''It has nothing to do with him where I work.''

''Except that he's a friend of yours and would like to be more than that, one gathers.''

On the pretext of examining one of the pictures on the wall, she turned her back on him. ''He's just a friend.''

He made no comment, and she added, ''I've only known him a few days longer than I have you.''

''You don't believe in what the romantics call love at first sight, then?''

Polly moved along to look at another picture. ''I don't know. I haven't really thought about it much.''

''Most girls of your age think of little else. Don't tell me you're a fervent careerist.''

''I don't think so, but I've been fairly busy in the last five years. One has to take life as it comes, I think.''

''Sometimes it comes without one realizing it.''

She shot a glance at him. ''Yes, I suppose so.''

There was another silence, and then he said idly, ''I imagine a doctor and a nurse are an excellent combination.''

Polly turned to face him, and for once she managed to look casual and unconcerned. "I didn't know men jumped to those sort of conclusions on so little evidence," she said with a smile. "You must be one of the romantics, although I wouldn't have thought it."

He refilled their glasses and lit a cigarette. "No, rather the reverse. But I don't believe in so-called platonic friendships, particularly when the man is young and impressionable and the girl is pretty and not too sure of her emotions."

"Are you psychoanalysing me again?"

"Merely warning you that young Barrington is more than half in love with you already, since it seems quite possible that you haven't recognized the signals," he said blandly.

"What signals? The fact that he was holding my hand when you came back?" she said tautly. "That isn't very conclusive nowadays. I don't know what goes on here, but in England people can hold hands without announcing their engagement the next day."

"My dear girl, if Barrington were an islander he wouldn't have been holding your hand, he'd have been kissing you," he said mockingly.

"Either way it would be my affair, wouldn't it?" she said pointedly.

His eyes narrowed and for an instant she had the feeling that he was angry with her. The impression was so strong that, involuntarily, she stepped back a pace.

Then he said quietly, "You look pale. You'd better run along. I'll tell Renata to have your breakfast served half an hour later tomorrow. Good night."

Polly stared at him for a moment and then, with a murmured good night, she slipped out of the room and ran upstairs.

MARISA WAS in such a fever of impatience to collect her kitten next day that Polly decided not to make her wait until the afternoon and asked Tonio if he could take them down to the village at ten, collecting Giles on the way back. He had already left the café when they stopped there and was halfway up the hill road by the time they caught up with him.

"Where does St. Clair go off to during the day?" he asked when they were down on the beach, shaded from the heat by a long stretch of blue canvas awning supported by posts at each corner.

Polly watched Marisa bending lovingly over her kitten, a blue-eyed handful of black and white fur that was unsteadily exploring the sand around it.

"He seems to have plenty to do," she said. "He explained the working of the estate to me the other day. Apparently it encloses what they call a *pieve,* that's a group of villages built fairly close to each other, at least as the crow flies. There's also quite a big vineyard beyond Maranza and a copper mine to the north that belongs to him."

"He doesn't run the castle and a yacht and a fleet of cars on the proceeds of a vineyard and a mine, I'll bet," Giles said knowingly.

"Oh no, he's away a good deal looking after some business interests in France. I think he has shares in a shipping company and some industrial concerns."

"Hm, sounds very cushy. I shall have to slog for everything I want," Giles said with a wry face.

"Have you always wanted to be a doctor?" she asked.

He gave her an impudent grin. "This is my idea of living. Lazing around in the sun with nothing to do and a couple of pretty girls for company."

"No, seriously."

"As seriously as you like, I'm a born idler."

"But being a doctor is terribly hard work, even at the consultant level," she said.

"You're telling me. I wouldn't mind so much if the grind eased off when I've qualified, but that's when the real toil and tear set in."

She stared at him. "You're are just pulling my leg, aren't you? I mean, medicine is a vocation. It isn't like ordinary jobs. One has to be... well, dedicated."

He knocked out his pipe and stuck it in the pocket of his beach shirt.

"Ah, there's the rub. I'm not the dedicated type."

"But why on earth are you studying for it if you aren't really keen?"

He stretched and rubbed the back of his neck. "The old man's dead keen for me to follow in his august footsteps and keeping him happy makes life easier. If I'd told him I wanted to be a tinker or tailor or what have you, he might have been nettled and decided to cut me off without the proverbial shilling."

"Was there something else that you did want to do?" she asked.

"Nope, not a thing."

"But, Giles, it's so important for a man to have a career that really interests him," she protested. "It's more than half his life."

He leaned foward to smile at Marisa and tickled the kitten, which was trying unsuccessfully to clamber up his ankle.

"It's not any more important than finding the right girl," he said over his shoulder. "That's the trouble at home. My father chose the wrong girl and then made things worse by neglecting her for his great vocation. Would you want to twiddle your thumbs every night while your husband kept his nose in some dry-as-dust treatise on neurology?"

"If I loved him I'd want him to achieve his ambitions," she said quietly.

"That's easy to say, but it doesn't always work out," he answered somberly. "Women need something to keep them happy, too, if it's only a jaunt to the flicks once a week."

"But people can't live on love indefinitely," she pointed out. "One has a home to make and children to bring up. That can't be done on thin air and kisses."

"Are you the kind who thinks a man should have some nice fat prospects lined up before he asks a girl to take a chance with him?" he asked.

"No, of course not. I wouldn't turn someone down because I knew they'd never be able to give me mink and diamonds. But I would want my husband to work for me and our children—and I'd want him to be happy in whatever he did."

He rested his elbows on his knees and looked down at the sand.

"It was a mistake to tell you that I wasn't burning with the urge to heal the world. I suppose it's put you off me."

"Why should it? I was only disturbed to think of you doing something you aren't really keen on. You'll probably find that once the study part is over and you're getting down to business, you want to be a doctor," she said encouragingly.

"Maybe. Anyway I'm not going to brood on it at the moment," he said, standing up. "How about a swim? Marisa will be okay for a while, won't she? The way she's stroking that kitten, it'll be bald before the week's out."

After lunch, Polly took the child upstairs for her siesta and then walked with Giles in the garden. The sun burned fiercely in the hot blue sky but a soft breeze from the sea made the temperature tolerable and the estate was much less enervating than low-lying Ajaccio.

"When do you have to go home?" she asked as they strolled along a grassy ride under tall pines.

"Not for three weeks."

"Are you going to rejoin your friends soon?"

"I don't think so. I can see Naples and die another year. Old Romanetti seems quite happy to put me up as long as I can pay the shot, so I'll probably stick around till it's time to get back. That's if you have no objections?"

"Of course not, it's nice for me to have a friend here," she said with a smile.

"What about you?" he asked. "How long are you staying?"

"I haven't thought about it. I think Marisa's apparent delicacy was ninety percent nervous trouble, and Raoul may decide to send her to school in Ajaccio or even France when he sees that she's really quite a strong child given the right handling."

"I didn't know you called him that. How long have you been on first-name terms?" Giles inquired with a hint of displeasure.

"Oh, not very long," she said evasively. "I wonder what that highest mountain is called?"

He glanced upward to the distant snow-capped peak that dominated the long range of lesser mountains forming the spine of the island.

"Monte d'Oro," he said briefly, then said, "I suppose from a woman's point of view he's quite a heart-throb, in spite of that gash on his face."

"Yes, possibly," Polly said in a detached tone, feeling that any discussion of Raoul was best avoided.

To her relief he did not pursue the topic and presently they returned to the castle where he said, "I suppose I'd better not outstay my welcome. He may not mind your having a 'follower' as they used to say, but I dare say he won't want me underfoot too often. No chance of your coming down to the village tonight, I suppose?"

"I don't think I will, Giles. I've some sewing to do and I want an early night if possible. I'll probably see you tomorrow unless you decide to go climbing."

"I'd rather be with you," he said softly.

When he was gone Polly went upstairs to find the kitten drowsing in the curve of Marisa's neck. It twitched a diminutive whisker as she came near the bed, but neither of them stirred, and she let them rest together until teatime.

Had Raoul been right when he said that Giles was more than half in love with her, she wondered. And if so, was it fair to go on seeing him unless she was beginning to feel the same way?

"I don't know. I honestly don't know," she said aloud to her reflection.

RENATA HAD unearthed the old sewing machine of which Raoul had spoken, so after dinner Polly retired to her room to work on Marisa's shorts. It was ten o'clock when she snipped the final thread and put them aside ready for pressing. While she was in the bathroom, someone had brought the glass of milk and plate of biscuits that were left on her bedside cabinet every night and, disinclined to go to bed yet, she took them to the window seat and sat listening to the murmur of the sea and breathing in the heady fragrance of the *dama de noche* on the terrace below.

Although the moon was up and pale stars spangled the deepening blueness of the sky, it was not yet dark. The stable clock was striking eleven when she stirred herself, padded into the bathroom to clean her teeth, and climbed into the big carved bed. But such a night was not made for sleeping and when the distant clock chimed the half hour, she was still turning restlessly from side to side, trying to shut out the scents and sounds that seemed to fill the room. At last, knowing it was useless to go on lying there, she flung back the covers and felt for her slippers. Five minutes later, a bathing suit under her dressing gown, she crept out into the corridor, her heart thumping a little from mingled nervousness and excitement.

The moonlight, flooding through the stained glass windows of the gallery, cast strange and eerie shadows in the hall below, and as a stair creaked under her foot she caught her breath and was tempted to fly back to bed. She was glad to reach the terrace. By night the castle seemed to stir with a life of its own, and it was easy to remember and believe Renata's stories of the turbulent past of the wraiths of forgotten centuries that still kept watch.

But climbing down the rocky stairway, because the elevator was locked up at night, she forgot these fancies in the softness of the scented air and the shimmer of the water below. The beach was still warm from the day's sun and quickly shrugging off her robe and tossing it on a rock, she ran across the sand to the sea's edge.

Although Raoul had told her that the sea outside the cove was always chilly even in high summer, the shallows lapping the sand felt tepid, and she stood knee-deep while she pulled on her bathing cap and made sure the flange was in place. She had often bathed after dark with Drew and the other boys, but never before alone, and for a moment she hesitated. Then after a neat duck dive, she struck out with the slow steady crawl that Drew had taught her when she was still in ankle socks, and headed toward the raft.

The calm tideless water was like silk against her limbs. Reaching the raft, she clung to the ropes for a few moments, and then, exhilarated by the sense of freedom of being at one with the sea and the sky, she turned on her back and floated. Presently she tried a few porpoise rolls and then a stretch of leisurely back stroke.

It was the sudden chilling of the water that made her discover, with surprise and the faintest prick of dismay, that she had swum much farther than she had meant to. She was quite close to the line of small rocks that ran out like the backbone of a sea serpent to the outer limits of the bay. The beach and above the dark bulk of the castle, looked a long way away.

After treading water for a minute, she began to swim back to the shore. She was really cold now and her arm muscles had begun to ache slightly so that her strokes were slower and less rhythmic. When she paused, thinking she must be quite close to the beach, she found she had still a good distance to go.

What happened next was one of the most frightening experiences of her life. Suddenly, in midkick, a sharp pain speared her right thigh and she floundered, swallowing water. As she choked on the salty mouthful and tried to get onto her back, she knew with horror and despair that the pain in her leg was a cramp. The next seconds had a nightmare quality. She knew that her only hope was to keep as still as possible and let the water support her until the spasm passed. But the pain was so agonizing that every muscle in her body seemed to contract, making her thrash out wildly.

And then as she gasped and spluttered and strained in a final convulsive effort not to go under, a dark shape reared out of the water near by and strong hands grasped her shoulders.

"Easy now, don't fight." One of the hands slid under her arm and the other cupped her chin.

Two minutes later she was flat on her back on the sand, gulping down air.

"No, don't sit up yet. There's no rush," Raoul said

presently, when her long shuddering breaths began to ease and she tried to raise herself.

Polly sank back on the sand and blinked the water out of her eyes, only vaguely aware that he was rubbing her cramped leg and that the pain had almost gone. For a while she lay still, too exhausted to move again or to speak. And then with her breath coming normally again and the stars no longer swinging dizzily above her, she began to tremble.

Raoul slipped an arm under her back, lifted her and propped her against his bent knee. Then wrapping a towel around her shaking shoulders, he felt for the catch of her bathing cap and pulled it off.

"I—I'm s-so s-sorry," Her teeth were chattering so much that the words were hardly intelligible.

"Just take it easy. You're quite safe now." He drew her against him, rubbing her back through the towel.

Too greatly shocked to have any normal reactions to this, Polly huddled against him, and then, the full significance of what she had escaped hitting her like a physical blow, burst into tears. She cried for several minutes, tears pouring down her cheeks, until quite suddenly the worst of the reaction passed and she sniffed and rubbed a hand over her eyes and said in a shaky but coherent voice, "Have you got a handkerchief, please?"

"Sorry, I didn't bring one. Mop up with the towel. I'll get your wrap."

He paused a moment to make sure sure she could sit up unsupported and then went up the beach to fetch her dressing gown. When he came back she was standing up, pale but steadied.

"Thank you. I'm sorry about all that," she said, putting it on.

He picked up her cap and took the towel. Then in silence they went up the beach toward the steps. At the foot of the flight he said, "Wait a moment," and as she turned he put one arm around her shoulder, the other under her knees, and swung her up against his chest.

"Oh, please...! I can walk...you can't possibly carry....", she began in confusion.

"Put your arm around my neck and hold on," he said briefly.

"But really I can. . ." Her protest trailed off and she did as he said.

Reaching the terrace, he set her on her feet and picked up a dark silk dressing gown flung carelessly over the balustrade.

"About 125 pounds, I would wager," he said, smiling at her.

"One hundred and twenty." She managed a wan smile back. "But I could have got up by myself."

He raked back his wet hair. "'Ingratitude, thou marble-hearted fiend.'"

"I'm sorry. It was very kind of you."

He pushed her toward the doorway. "Go and get that wet suit off and don't hang around before getting into bed. I don't want to have to fetch the doctor for you."

Polly hesitated. How did one thank a man for saving one's life? Then as he snapped his fingers at her she turned and went quickly inside.

Back in her room, she stripped off the wet suit, toweled vigorously, picked up her flimsy nylon pajamas that her mother had insisted she should bring. It took a few minutes to find where Constancia had put them, but once on they made her feel more human. Without bothering to rinse out her swimsuit, she climbed into bed and turned off the lamp.

A few minutes later, longing for a hot-water bottle, she sat up and reached for the embroidered quilt that was folded into a neat strip at the foot of the bed. She was tucking it around her when there was a tap at the door. Lighting the lamp again, she called, "Come in."

"I thought you might feel like an extra blanket," Raoul said, closing the door behind him. "Sorry if you'd already dropped off, but it took me some time to find this." He indicated the old-fashioned earthenware bed warmer he was carrying.

"Oh, a bottle!" Polly said eagerly. "Just what I was longing for."

He gave it to her and shook out the blanket he had

brought. "Rather an antiquated specimen, I'm afraid, but we don't often need them."

She thrust it under the bedclothes and maneuvered it down to her feet.

"I'd have welcomed a warming pan. My feet are icy," she said gratefully.

As he finished arranging the blanket, he noticed the diaphanous nightdress •draped over a chair and glanced at her pajamas.

"That was sensible of you."

She looked up at him, suddenly shy. "I've been wondering how to thank you. It was lucky for me you were around. Otherwise...." She shivered.

"I generally take a late dip, and I was in the study when I heard you creaking down the stairs. Don't worry about it, it's unlikely to happen again. I expect you were tired and went out too far." He produced a small silver flask and poured a generous measure of its contents into the water glass on the cabinet. "Try a tot of this to complete the cure. It's only rum."

She sipped it cautiously, disliking the taste but welcoming any source of warmth. He watched her, his hands in the pockets of the dressing gown, his glance impersonal.

"If you hadn't come, I would be drowned by now," she said suddenly in a low voice.

He sat down on the side of the bed. "Don't think about it. Forget it. Next time I'll come with you."

"I don't think there'll be a next time."

"We'll see. Warmer?"

She nodded, wishing that it was daytime so that she would not be left alone until the memory of that struggle in the water had faded a little.

"It's time you were asleep," he said. "Like another tot to help you get off?"

She shook her head. "I'll be all right now. And thank you again."

He pocketed the flask, his eyes amused.

"Your head is stronger than I would have suspected. I

was hoping a good-sized drink would keel you over right away.''

Polly leaned back against the pillows. ''I do feel a bit hazy,'' she admitted.

''Good. Then I'm not risking a painful rebuff.''

She stared at him, not understanding what he was talking about.

''For this,'' he said, and leaning forward he kissed her lightly on the mouth. ''There, that should give you something more cheerful to think about. Goodnight. Sweet dreams,'' he said teasingly.

Before she could recover from her stupefaction, he had flicked off the lamp and gone quietly out of the room.

As SHE DRANK her early morning tea and nibbled a *petit beurre,* Polly was inclined to think that it had all been a dream fantasy. But the extra blanket and the stone bottle, now almost cold, were proof that everything had happened just as the remembered.

Yet, as she bathed and dressed, she was not obsessed by her nearly fatal accident, but by that moment when a little muddled by shock and neat rum, she had seen Raoul bend over her and not realized till the very last second what he intended. Surprisingly, she had slept almost at once. But now, clearheaded again, she remembered the light pressure of his lips and his parting shot with an odd tightness inside her.

As lunchtime drew near she wished she had some excuse for avoiding him and, as she followed Marisa onto the terrace, her cheeks were hot with embarrassment. Her confusion proved to be unnecessary, however, as he was in an unusually abstracted and taciturn mood and scarcely glanced at her.

Three uneventful days after her calamitous moonlight swim, Polly was standing in the hall reading a second letter from her mother that had just arrived by way of a grubby urchin from the village, when a car drew up outside. Quick light footsteps crossed the gravel and clicked up the steps. The enormous black bell that hung above the entrance jangled resoundingly and a moment later a young girl strolled into the hall.

For some seconds they stared at each other: the visitor seeming mildly surprised and Polly looking stunned. For the girl who had clanged the bell and sauntered inside was one of the most breathtaking creatures she had ever seen.

She was about eighteen or nineteen, with a perfect oval face, glossy black hair and soft dark eyes fringed by incredibly long lashes. Not only was she ravishingly lovely, but her clothes were of the kind that any fashion-conscious woman would recognize at a glance as coming from the most exclusive and expensive shops. The simple white chemise dress, which somehow contrived to have the latest unfitted lines and yet reveal her apparently faultless figure, reached to just below her knees, and her long slim legs were veiled in the palest of pale green stockings to tone with her green suède slippers. A hip-length rope of jade beads was twisted around her shapely throat and her gloves and bag were white suede. To complete the vision of elegance, a garland of green and white leaves and tulle was set on her beautifully dressed hair.

They were still surveying each other when the study door opened and Raoul appeared.

"Raoul!"

With a a cry of delight, the strange girl flung herself into his arms.

Polly was still too stunned to be capable of discreetly fading away and could only stand and gape at this whirl-wind greeting.

But after a second or two, her employer extricated himself from the girl's enthusiastic embrace and, wiping her lipstick off his cheek, said indulgently. "So you're back, are you? I thought tomorrow was the great day."

"Oh, I suppose papa muddled the dates as usual. He never reads my letters properly, anyway," the girl said, laughing.

"Probably because your handwriting is so atrocious, *petite*," Raoul said with a grin. Then, turning to Polly, "This is Antonetta Rivera, Polly. The girl who can't drive. Tonetta, this is Miss Linsey."

The girl turned to Polly, a warm smile parting her full red lips and revealing perfect teeth.

"How do you do, Miss Linsey," she said charmingly. "Papa told me about you, but I expected someone quite old with gray stockings and a little stiff cap, you know. How nice for Marisa that you are young and pretty, and—" with a mischievous glance at St. Clair "—for Raoul, too!"

Polly smiled, trying not to show the embarrassment that this sally produced.

"It will be nice for me, also," Antonetta went on. "There are no girls of our age near here, you see. Now I shall be able to come over and have lovely long talks instead of sitting alone so much."

"Polly has more to do than to listen to your chatter all day, *ma mie*," Raoul said dryly. "Another thorn in her side may be too much."

"A thorn?" the girl said, puzzled. Then thinking she grasped what he meant asked, "Oh, you don't like Corsica too much, Miss Linsey? That is easy to understand. It is all right for old people and children, but not for girls. Even Ajaccio is like a small town where everyone knows everyone else. I prefer Paris where one can meet all kinds of interesting people and go to cheerful places and have fun."

"I'm beginning to wonder if I should have persuaded your father to let you go," Raoul said.

Twin dimples appeared at the corners of her mouth and her eyes glinted with provocative laughter. "Don't you think I have improved?"

His glance ranged from the frivolous hat to her slim ankles and then returned to her face. "In some respects."

Antonetta pretended to be piqued. "In Corsica men only approve of women who want to cook and sew and have babies," she said to Polly. "In France it is very different. Frenchmen are so charming, so gallant. They know how to pay compliments, but if you show your new hat to a man here he just grunts at you like a pig."

"You forget, actions speak louder than words." Raoul said dryly.

Antonetta giggled wickedly. "Yes, I know. Frenchmen are very good at actions, also."

He laughed at her. "So you've been learning other things besides painting your face and walking on those ridiculous heels, have you? Nicole is obviously much too lenient a chaperone."

"Nicole says that girls should have flirtations before they settle down to marriage," Antonetta informed him gravely. "Otherwise how will they know who is the right man for them?"

"And what if your father has already chosen an estimable husband for you?" he asked, watching her with an odd expression.

She dimpled again. "Then you will have to persuade him to let me choose whom I please."

His mouth twitched, but Polly fancied that his eyes were serious.

"I might agree with his choice," he said. "However, that is a matter for the future. Come and have something to refresh you. I want to hear how Nicole is getting on. Will you join us, Polly?"

"Thank you, but I was just going up to wake Marisa," she said.

"We'll see you later, then," he said.

Polly nodded, smiled at Antonetta and walked to the stairs. In her room she crossed to the window. The sea was almost emerald in the afternoon light and the breeze was sweet with the scent of the *maquis*. Yet, for no reason at all, she felt dull and downcast, as if a shadow had fallen on the golden day.

CHAPTER FIVE

WHEN, HALF AN HOUR later, Polly took Marisa down to the yellow salon to greet their visitor, she found Antonetta curled up on one of the sofas, chattering away in rapid French. But as soon as they entered the Corsican girl broke off what she was saying and held out her hands to the child.

"Raoul, would you fetch the parcel that I left in the back of the car, please?" she asked. "It is a present for *la petite*. Can you guess what I have brought you from Paris, *chérie?*"

Marisa shook her head, plainly fascinated by the long jade necklace, the coral-painted nails and the misty green stockings. Antonetta must always have been a delight to look at, Polly thought, but evidently her extreme elegance had been acquired during her stay in Paris.

Raoul was back within a few moments bringing a large beribboned box. Marisa's eyes widened and she needed no urging to open it. Inside was a large doll with platinum curls and eyelashes that were even longer and thicker than Antonetta's. The doll was dressed in a blue velvet coat trimmed with white fur over a blue silk dress, and the box also contained a miniature suitcase packed with a playsuit, a blouse and skirt and a ballet dress.

"Oh, Polly, look! She has a suspender belt just like yours, and real stockings!" Marisa exclaimed delightedly, investigating the doll's underwear. "Oh, and look, dear little gloves!"

"She's lovely," Polly agreed. "Aren't you going to thank Miss Rivera?"

Marisa turned a glowing face to their guest. "Thank you very much," she said gravely.

"You must think of a name for her," Antonetta said happily, pleased with the success of her gift.

Marisa considered this important matter for a minute. "I'll call her Prunella—like the little girl in our story, Polly," she said, looking at her nurse for approval of this choice.

"Shouldn't she have a French name as she's a French doll?" Polly suggested.

"No, I want to call her Prunella," Marisa said firmly. "May I take her coat off?" This she asked Antonetta.

"Of course, *petite*. You may do whatever you like. She is yours."

"I think I'll take her upstairs and introduce her to Paolo. May I, Polly?"

"Yes, of course, I'll come with you," Polly said.

"No, stay and have a drink. Marisa can perform the introduction by herself, I daresay," Raoul put in. "Off you go, baggage. Don't let Prunella fall down the stairs."

So, clutching the doll to her chest, Marisa went off to present the china-faced Parisienne to her kitten, and Polly was obliged to stay behind.

"But what a change in her," Antonetta remarked when the door had closed. "She was always so pale and quiet and a package of nerves. You are very good for her, Miss Linsey."

"She's very easy to manage. I think she was a little lonely before," Polly replied.

"You like this work—guarding *les enfants*?"

"Yes, I love it. I never wanted to do anything else."

"I expect you will soon have many babies of your own," said Antonetta. "Oh, how fortunate the English are. In Corsica it is not considered proper for girls to have, what is it called—a career—before they are married. We have no freedom. Our parents keep watch on us until we are chosen in marriage, and then it is no better because our husbands are very jealous and have always the fear that we look at another man."

Raoul handed Polly a glass of wine. "Yes, poor child, you are the epitome of your grossly underprivileged sex,'' he said satirically, with a glance that took in the cigarette holder with which she punctuated her remarks, the vivid young mouth and the shapely pair of knees that her short skirt exposed.

She laughed and wrinkled her nose at him. "I was not including you," she retorted. "You are not old-fashioned and cross with me when I want to be happy and enjoy life." She turned to Polly. "It is a very good mixture—the English and the Corsican. He is not stern, always saying 'No, you must not do this. It is not correct behavior *pour une jeune fille bien élevée.*' But he is also very much a man, and that is more exciting than one who is much too easy to manage, is it not?"

Polly forced a thin smile, carefully avoiding Raoul's eyes.

"Are you on holiday or have you come home for good, Miss Rivera?" she asked.

"*Hélas,* I must stay here now," Antonetta answered regretfully. "But at least I have had one year of happy times, and I would not have had that if Raoul had not assured papa that it would be good for me. Now I must wait for someone to marry me. But—" with a demure downward sweep of her lashes and the suspicion of a smile "—perhaps it will not be too long."

Polly could not help glancing at Raoul to see his reaction to this remark.

But although he was watching the younger girl his expression was unreadable.

Presently Antonetta swung her legs to the floor and said she must be off. "Papa would like you to dine with us tomorrow, Raoul. It will be a small party for my homecoming. He would also like to meet Miss Linsey, if she will accept."

"You haven't made a date with Barrington for tomorrow night, have you, Polly?" he asked.

She shook her head. "No, but—"

"Then tell your father we shall both be delighted to attend," he said to Antonetta. "About seven-thirty?"

"Yes. We are dining at eight o'clock and there will be a dance later—for those of the guests who are not too

old," she added, with a wry face. "No, don't come out
with me, Raoul. If you are watching me I shall not be
able to make the car work. *Au revoir,* Miss Linsey. I am
so glad to have met you."

And blowing a kiss to Raoul she turned and swayed
gracefully to the door, turning to throw him a final
naughtily coquettish smile before she disappeared.

Raoul chuckled. "She was always a minx," he said.
"I'm afraid a year in Paris hasn't had the chastening ef-
fect her father hoped for."

Polly looked down at her glass. "She's incredibly
lovely to look at," she said.

There was a pause, then he said quietly, "You really
do admire her, don't you?"

"Well, naturally. How could anyone not?"

"Few people will," he said dryly. "To the single ones
she'll be unfair competition and to the matrons a poten-
tial third party in the ancient triangle."

"I wouldn't say that. Women don't inevitably resent
someone who is better looking than they are. It's only if
a woman is beautiful and also grasping and unscrupulous that they are wary of her. I'm sure Mademoiselle
Rivera is not like that."

"No, she isn't. By rare chance her nature is just as
engaging as her looks. But I fancy that won't save her
from the barrage of feminine jealousy. Your views on
the subject aren't too representative."

He smoked in silence for a time, then said, "You
didn't seem very enthusiastic about the invitation for
tomorrow night."

"I thought she might have included me out of politeness. After all I'm not a houseguest here."

"Neither are you a kitchen maid," he said briefly.
"Don't tell me you're an inverted snob."

"Not that I'm aware. I just don't want to intrude in a
gathering of old friends."

"You won't."

She hesitated. "Will it be very formal—full evening
dress?" she asked.

"I wouldn't think so. The women will probably wear

short cocktail dresses or whatever they're called. Have you got something suitable, or d'you want to run down to Ajaccio, again?''

"No, I have a dress that should do," she said. "I think I'd better go up and see how Prunella and Paolo are getting along."

He moved to open the door for her, and without looking at him, she murmured a word of thanks and left the room.

THE FOLLOWING EVENING, a few minutes before the time that Raoul had asked her to be ready to leave for the Riveras' house farther along the coast, Polly stood before the mirror in her room and inspected her reflection. She was wearing a dress of stiff cream moiré silk with narrow shoulder straps, a close-fitting waist and a skirt that fell straight at the front and was draped in a kind of bustle at the back. She had bought it for a Rugger Club dance at home a year ago, and her mother and several friends had told her that it was the most becoming dress she had ever had, but remembering the unmistakable haute couture stamp of Antonetta's clothes the previous afternoon, she did not feel particularly confident in it tonight.

"Why are you looking so sad, Polly?" Marisa asked, watching her from the couch where she was cuddling Prunella in one arm and Paolo in the other.

Polly smiled at her. "Not really sad," she said. "I was just wondering which earrings to wear. What do you think, the pearl studs or these green ones?"

Marisa considered them gravely. "The green ones," she advised. "They're like darling little waterfalls, all cool and glittery."

Polly obediently fixed the green earrings to her lobes. They were made of strands of the most minute green and silver beads falling in small cascades from the hidden clips. Since there were more flamboyant than most of her jewelry she decided to wear no other ornaments.

"You will make sure that Prunella has a good supper and goes to sleep quickly, won't you?" she said, picking up the stole to match the dress and a small silk theater purse. ''We won't be late back and I'll creep in to have a look at all of you before I go to bed.''

Marisa promised to see that her doll and kitten behaved themselves and after kissing all three good-night, Polly left them to await Constancia's arrival with the supper.

Raoul was in the hall when she reached the staircase and she had to walk all the way down it with his eyes on her.

''I hope this will do,'' she said, adjusting her stole.

''Very well,'' he said briefly. ''Shall we go?''

As she climbed into the Jaguar and arranged her skirts to avoid creasing them as much as possible, she could not help feeling that he might have said she looked nice or made some encouraging remark instead of that terse ''Very well.'' Perhaps it didn't occur to him that meeting a group of strangers, especially of a different nationality, could be an ordeal to someone who did not share his own impregnable self-assurance.

It took them half an hour to reach the Rivera's house, and throughout the drive Raoul was silent and withdrawn. But when he had parked the car alongside several others already at the head of the short drive, he helped her out and kept his hand on her arm.

''There will probably be a number of eligible youngsters here tonight,'' he said. ''Be careful with that wide-eyed smile of yours. They are more romantically inclined than most English youths and might misinterpret it. I don't want to have to rescue you from too many advances.''

''That's not very likely with Miss Rivera on the scene,'' she said.

His hands dropped. ''You have the advantage of being a novelty,'' he returned. ''Black-eyed beauties are the rule here; that English coloring has the allure of the exotic. Don't tell me later that I should have warned you.''

The house, although insignificant compared with Castel Maranza, was spacious and richly furnished.

Their host, a tall spare man in his late fifties, was waiting to welcome them at the door of a long tessellated salon. He gave Polly a polite but shrewd scrutiny as Raoul presented her, and then bowed over her hand and said courteously. "We are delighted to welcome you, my child. I hope to have the pleasure of a talk later in the evening."

Antonetta, who was standing beside him in a dress of flame chiffon and rhinestones at her ears and wrists, greeted Polly equally warmly and then, leaving the two men to talk for a moment, whisked her off to be introduced to the other guests. These were mainly contemporaries of her father, but there was one other young girl and three or four dark-haired men of around Polly's age.

When not long afterward the company adjourned to the dining room, Polly found herself seated between two of these "eligible youths" and as they both helped to draw out her chair, she caught Raoul's eye on her from farther along the table and saw his mouth twitch.

At the end of the meal the women withdrew to a second and smaller salon to take coffee, leaving the men to "talk about politics and dull business matters" as Antonetta put it. However, it was not more than twenty minutes or so before they heard voices emerging from the dining room, and then everyone returned to the main salon and the older guests ranged themselves around the walls to gossip, while the younger set prepared to dance. The arrival of some more people who had not been able to come to dinner brought the number of girls up to six and, to her astonishment, Polly soon discovered that she was the most in demand as a partner. With Antonetta looking like some exquisite scarlet flower, Polly could not fathom why, within the bounds of politeness to herself and the other girls, they were not all clustering around their host's radiant daughter. It was not until one of the young men begged her to permit him to escort her around the garden and she could find no adequate reason for refusing the suggestion that she discovered the reason for their apparent immunity to Antonetta's charms.

As they returned toward the glass doors that extended across the whole of one end of the salon, they saw Antonetta dancing past in the arms of one of the older guests.

She was smiling up at him, her eyes as starry as the jewels at her ears, her filmy skirt floating out behind her.

"How pretty she is," Polly said.

"Oh, yes, she is a charming girl—although to many the English rose is fairer than our Corsican orchid," her escort said gallantly.

Polly remembered Raoul's warning and although she thought it exaggerated, she did not smile at the compliment.

"I have offended you?" the young man asked anxiously. "You do not want me to express my admiration?"

She bit her lip wondering what she could say that would not sound ungracious.

"Ah, I understand. It is the customary misfortune," he said quickly, before she could answer. "As in the case with Antonetta, your affections are already engaged, no? My apologies, I had hoped it was otherwise."

It was a second or two before the significance of what he had said sank in.

"You mean Antonetta is engaged?" Polly asked.

He shrugged. "That I cannot say. If so, it is known only to the family. I think there is no formal betrothal, yet. But—" with a wry expression "—she makes it clear that it is of no use to pay court to her. You must forgive me, Mademoiselle Polly. I would not have asked you to walk with me had I known that you were betrothed, although I understand your customs in these matters are less strict than in Corsica."

Polly agreed that they were, seeing no purpose in correcting his mistaken assumption that she was engaged. So Antonetta was in love with someone, she thought, as they went inside. These men knew it, and that was why they didn't attempt to compete for her favor.

It also gave new meaning to the seemingly careless remark that she had made yesterday afternoon about Raoul persuading her father to allow her to marry the man of her choice. What was it Raoul had answered? *"I might agree with his choice. However, that is a matter for the future."*

"May I have this dance, Polly?"

She came out of her reverie to find the subject of her thoughts smiling down at her. Automatically she smiled and accepted his outstretched hand. Like most tall lithe men, Raoul had a relaxed uncomplicated style that was easy to follow. At first he held her lightly, a little away from him. Then, as the first number on the long-playing record came to an end and the orchestra launched into a nostalgic waltz, his arms tightened and he drew her closer. Fighting against a reasonless instinct to resist the firm pressure of his hand against her back, Polly told herself that people often danced as closely as this and that if the dancing area had been more crowded she would not even have noticed the alteration. She tried to pretend that it was Drew or Giles who held her, that it was Drew's cheek that brushed her temple as they swung into a turn, Drew's muscular arm beneath her fingers. The device was not successful. With every beat of the music her pulse quickened, and she grew more disturbingly aware that the man holding her so close to him was neither her brother nor Giles. By the time the record ended her cheeks were hot and it was an effort to look unconcerned.

"Thank you. Would you care for another turn in the garden?" he asked.

Before she could reply, he had placed her left hand on his sleeve and led her outside.

"Dancing is a curious custom when one considers it," he said presently, as they walked along the paved pathway that circled the lawn.

Polly removed her hand from his arm.

"Yes, I suppose to people who had never seen any before, it would look rather peculiar," she agreed, "or, at any rate, the ballroom kind would. Most races have some kind of folk dancing, don't they?"

"The point of ballroom dancing is fairly obvious," he said casually. "It's only an excuse for holding a girl who isn't normally approachable to that extent—and vice versa."

"Not vice versa," Polly said coolly. "Quite often girls have to dance with men they haven't the least inclination to be held by."

He smiled at her. "That was a pretty biting comeback. Has that first tour of the grounds made you edgy?"

"Not at all, Monsieur de Calla was charming."

"I don't doubt it. Did he kiss you?"

"Of course not," she said hotly. "I'm sure it never occurred to him."

"He's a most singular lad if he didn't," he said lazily. "Why the heated objection? Don't you like being kissed?"

She remembered the touch of his lips on the night of her bathe and her hands clenched.

"If I hadn't been upset and had that beastly rum, I'd have—"

"You'd have what?" he cut in. "Blacked my eye for me? Flung the hot-water bottle at my head?"

Polly's temper rose. "If you weren't so utterly despicable you wouldn't drag it up," she flared.

"But then I have never pretended to be the soul of honor, have I?" he said carelessly.

She swallowed, trying desperately to be calm. "I'm sorry. I shouldn't have said that. But you seem to...to delight in taunting me," she said.

"Probably because it interests me to watch that mask of polite reserve drop now and then. You don't let it slip very often. As it happens I wasn't even thinking of the particular incident that you evidently found so distasteful. Shall we get back to the others? I'm sure you'll feel safer in a crowd."

Several times before she had felt but not been certain that he was angry with her. This time there was no doubt. As he crossed the grass at her side his mouth was compressed in a grim line and his eyes were as cold and hard as a winter sea. As soon as they entered the salon, he steered her toward Antonetta and then excused himself.

Feeling that she could not possibly cope with party conversation for a few minutes, Polly asked her hostess if she could freshen up, and the younger girl showed her to a bedroom.

"You don't mind if I do not stop to chat just now, but I think old Madame Lascetti will be leaving in a moment and I must be there to say goodbye," Antonetta said.

Polly smiled and shook her head, only too glad to be alone for a while. When she had combed her hair and renewed her lipstick, she sat on the edge of the bed and thought dully that her truce with Raoul had been even briefer than she had expected. This time the breach of amity was her fault. He had only meant to tease her, which she ought to be used to by now. But instead of taking it lightly, she had flared up and made him think her even more of an idiot than he had before.

"...*the particular incident that you evidently found so distasteful.*" The inflexion he had used on those words made her wince. And it wasn't true. She had accepted the kiss for what it was—a deliberate attempt to take her mind off all that had gone before. Too late, she thought of all the things she might have said instead of flaring up at him: a dozen harmless rejoinders that would not have precipitated a row.

The drive home passed in an even more painful silence than the outward trip, and when they reached the castle Polly did not wait for him to help her out of the car, but muttered an indistinct good-night and fled up the steps.

Lying in bed, she faced the unalterable truth that she would never be able to get on with Raoul for any length of time. She was just not capable of handling his caustic humor. Only two kinds of women could hope to keep the peace with him. Those who would meekly allow him to goad them and those whose personalities were as direct and forceful as his own. *And I don't fit into either* category, she thought wretchedly. *Perhaps I ought to go home. But how can I when Marisa needs me so much?*

Her thoughts turned to Antonetta. Was Raoul the man with whom she was believed to be in love? It would not be so very surprising. He had obviously known the family all his life and next to her father was the man most closely associated with Antonetta from her school-days. What could be more natural than that she should fall in love with him? Particularly as he had everything to offer a women and yet was less narrow in his outlook than most of her circle.

And what about him? Was he in love with Antonetta? Was he capable of loving any woman? Perhaps love did not come into it. Perhaps he would marry her because she was beautiful and wellborn and intelligent, an ideal consort for the liege lord of Maranza. Certainly he did not behave like a man in love. Or was the indulgent elder-brother manner a screen to keep the truth from everyone until he chose to announce it?

Oh, what has it got to do with me anyway, Polly thought angrily, thumping her pillows. And her last, thought before sleep finally claimed her was, *Thank heaven for Giles.*

A WEEK PASSED. Three mornings Giles came down to the beach with them, Polly taking care not to swim out of her depth for fear her attack of cramp should recur, and three evenings she went down to the village to sit in a café and talk or go for a stroll with him. Raoul dined twice with the Riveras and, one afternoon at the end of the week, Antonetta came over and finding him out on the estate stayed to chat with Polly.

"Oh dear, how hot it is today," the Corsican girl said, unbuttoning her fuchsia linen skirt to reveal a pair of matching shorts. "I am used to our climate, but I do not like it as well as the cooler weather in Paris. Here one can never wear furs or velvets and wools, only cottons and silks that become so boring, don't you think? Me, I would like to live in a beautiful coat of white mink with a hat of violets."

"You look very nice all the same," said Polly, admiring the black and white shirt and white sandals that completed Antonetta's outfit.

"Raoul says I am frivolous to think so much about clothes," the other girl said with a laugh. "I tell him there are only three things a woman wishes to think of— love, clothes and nice things to eat. Have you had many *affaires de coeur,* Polly?"

"No, none at all, I'm afraid," Polly admitted, looking up from some mending to watch Marisa chasing Paolo around a tree.

"But Raoul tells me that you have a suitor who is staying in Maranza, a handsome doctor with red hair."

"Giles isn't a suitor. He's just a friend. And he's only studying to be a doctor."

"Ah, that makes it difficult. It will be a long time before he has enough money for a wife, I expect," Antonetta remarked. "You say he is only a friend. Don't you want him to be in love with you?"

"Not unless I am in love with him."

"No, it is very distressing to have to break someone's heart," Antonetta agreed soberly. "In Paris I knew a man who said he would kill himself if I did not marry him. I do not think he meant it, of course, because men often say foolish things when they are in love. But it was not nice to think of such a thing happening and I was very troubled by him for a long time. This boy who is not yet a doctor, is he very good too look at?"

"Yes, in a way. I wouldn't call him handsome, but he has a very pleasant face."

"Me, I prefer men who are very dark," Antonetta said. "They must be tall—because with a little man one cannot wear high heels—and strong and have perfect teeth. I do not want to sleep with a man who puts his teeth into a glass of water each night, not until he is quite old when it cannot be helped, of course. And blue eyes, he must have very blue eyes that will say 'I love you' when he looks at me." She gave a dreamy sigh and lay back in her chair, her eyes half-closed.

So it is Raoul she loves, Polly thought, with a strange

pang. *But does he tell her he loves her with his eyes, or is she only hoping that he will?*

Antonetta's lids lifted and she said, "You know, Polly, when I was first in Paris I did not want to get married because it seemed so dull to cook and sew and have babies. But now it is different. When one is in love one wants to do all these things. Raoul thinks I am silly and too young to settle down, but I am not, really I am not. I want to be settled, I want to be a good wife. Why cannot men understand these things? They are so blind."

Polly's mending fell to her lap. *So he knows that she loves him,* she thought. *He knows and he's putting her off by saying she's too young. Does he really believe that, or is it an excuse? Oh no, he couldn't be so cruel! He couldn't let her fall in love with him just for amusement. He couldn't!* Aloud, she said, "Yes, I know they are. But you are awfully young, Antonetta. Are you sure it will last? Sometimes one feels something intensely and then, after a time, it fades and one realizes that it was a mistake."

Antonetta looked up into the branches of the tree under which they were sitting. "I do not think this will fade," she said softly. "I think it will last all my life."

For a few moments her lovely face was illumined by a look of such softness and passionate longing that Polly wondered how anyone could mistake her happiness and charm for an essentially shallow and changeable nature. And then, almost as if she regretted her confidences, Antonetta stretched her arms above her head and laughed and said, "But I must not bore you with my troubles. It is as Raoul says, you look so gentle and sympathetic that one feels you will understand everything."

"Did Raoul really say that about me?" Polly said dryly.

"But yes. He has great admiration for you. He says that you are sometimes prim, that is a word I do not understand, but I think it is not a compliment, and that you are afraid of yourself, that again I do not understand. But he also says that you are very loyal and have much courage in other matters."

"How kind of him," Polly said in a blank tone.

Antonetta studied her for some seconds. "Perhaps I should not say this, but sometimes I think you do not like Raoul very much," she said. "The night you came to dine with us and he took you into the garden after dancing with you: that night you did not look happy, and Raoul, too, was angry."

"I expect we had an argument about something," Polly said as casually as she could manage. "We don't always see eye to eye on certain matters."

"Eye to eye?" Antonetta queried.

"It means that we don't agree."

"Oh yes, now I understand. He wishes you to say 'Yes, Raoul' all the time, and you will not." She laughed. "Papa says that Raoul is like the granite of our cliffs, but that one day he will become soft and gentle. Ah, here he is now."

Polly turned her head and saw her employer riding out of the woods, his crop raised to return Antonetta's wave.

"I'd forgotten. I mean to wash Marisa's hair this afternoon. We had better do it now," she said hastily, gathering her sewing together. By the time Raoul had reached the tree, she had called the child to her and was halfway across the lawn to the castle.

AT TEATIME Marisa complained of a sore throat and pushed her bread and butter away from her.

"Oh, darling, I wish you'd told me your throat hurt before I washed your hair," Polly said. "Never mind, it wasn't wet too long and you may feel better in the morning. All the same I think we'll pop you into bed straight away."

The child's temperature was normal and her forehead was cool and dry, so Polly did not feel unduly anxious about her. But as dinnertime drew near, she rang for Constancia and asked to have her meal brought upstairs, sending a note to Raoul to explain that Marisa was slightly off-color and that she would stay with her until she was asleep.

Shortly after the table clock had struck eight, Polly was writing to her mother and Marisa was sleeping, when there was a soft but urgent tattoo on the door. Closing her writing case she went to see who it was.

"Come outside a moment," Raoul said quietly as soon as she opened the door. He waited until she had shut it behind her, then said briskly, "Will it be all right to leave Constancia with her for a couple of hours?"

"Yes, of course, she's not actually ill. But why?"

"I've just had word from the village that there's been an accident and you may be useful. You know the goats go up into the hills to graze every morning. About an hour ago one of the herds found its own way home—without the boy who keeps an eye on them. Something has obviously happened to him. He's been climbing about the crags and fallen, I expect. We've known it before. Barrington has already gone off with the lad's father to see if they can find him, but when they do they'll almost certainly need help to get him back. It's possible he's seriously injured, in which case your nursing experience may be vital."

Polly did not waste time asking questions. "I'll get the first-aid box. I doubt if Giles has any equipment. I'll be down in two minutes," she said.

Less than five minutes later they were roaring down the drive in the jeep, with Polly squeezed between Raoul and Tonio and coils of rope and a tarpaulin in the back.

"Giles is still only a student and I'm not a hospital nurse. What about a doctor?" she asked anxiously.

"He's already out on a difficult maternity case," Raoul said. "The village he's gone to is a good hour's trip by mule track, so you two will have to do the best you can. It may only be a broken ankle or concussion." He looked at the sun that was slowly dropping behind the mountains. "The light will hold for a couple of hours yet, which is one godsend. These rescue jobs are the very devil after dark."

After jerking and jolting over ground that only a jeep could cover, with Raoul cursing under his breath whenever it looked as if they were going to get stuck, they reached the area where the herd was known to graze. A few seconds after they had scrambled out, they heard a loud halloo from somewhere above them and, looking up, saw Giles and another man waving urgently from the top of a steep rock-strewn slope. Fortunately Polly had been wearing flat-heeled shoes when Raoul called her, and with him hauling her over the worst places by brute strength and Tonio ready to shove behind, it did not take them long to reach the top.

"Good girl! I was counting on you having the sense to bring some first-aid gear," Giles said rapidly, reaching down to help heave her over the final wall of rock. Then turning to Raoul he said, "The boy is stuck on a narrow ledge halfway up that face. We'll have to operate from the top. I'll go down and see what shape he's in while you're rigging whatever sort of sling you can manage. If he's badly smashed up it may be touch and go, but we have no alternative. You won't be able to make it, Polly, so stay here until we get him down." He glanced at the boy's father, who was a grizzled man in his sixties with a large paunch. "He won't, either. Try to make him understand that we'll do our best."

To Polly, watching from below, it seemed an eternity before the three men reached the summit of the great bluff, but at last they did so and disappeared. The ledge where the boy was just visible, one leg dangling out of small bush that had evidently saved him from falling the full height of the cliff, was some distance to the left of the route the men had taken. Waiting for them to reappear, Polly put a comforting hand on the father's arm and felt him shaking, although his face was set and expressionless. Presently she saw Giles sitting on the edge of the clifftop, and a moment later he let himself over the top. Although she could see that there was a stout rope around his waist, she held her breath as he lowered himself downwards.

The ledge where the boy was lying was so narrow that it seemed impossible that he could attend to the lad's injuries, but after another interminable wait she saw him signal to his helpers, who then let down a kind of rough

hammock made from tarpaulin. Twenty minutes later
the boy was lying on the turf below the bluff with Giles
bending over him and the father kneeling by his son's
head with a silver crucifix clutched in his horny hands.

By this time several other villagers had arrived with a
homemade stretcher, and when Giles stood up and said,
"Well, that's the best I can do until we get him home,"
many willing hands were ready to ease him gently onto
it.

It was dusk when they reached the village and passed
through a crowd of weeping women and silent men into
the cottage where the boy's brothers and sisters were
huddling in a corner of the main room, their eyes wide
with alarm.

Sometime later Giles straightened from bending over
the meal table where the boy had been laid, passed his
forearm across his eyes and said, "Well that's as far as
we go. I hope it's far enough. You go on home, Polly.
I'll stay with him until the local man gets here."

"Are you sure there's nothing more I can do?"

"Yes, certain. You might come down in the morning.
The mother doesn't seem to have much sense and the
place could do with a cleanup. See you then."

Polly looked at him and wondered how it was possible for people to change so much in the space of a few
hours. Then reaching up she kissed him softly on the
cheek and slipped out of the door.

Raoul was waiting for her outside. "We could take
him down to Ajaccio if Barrington wants it," he said.

She shook her head. "No, I think he's going to be all
right. Giles is sure there are no internal injuries."

He nodded and helped her to climb back into the
jeep. It was not until they were out of the village that he
said, "Barrington should make a pretty good doctor.
He took charge of the situation like an old hand."

She smiled to herself. "Yes, I think he should."

MARISA'S SORE THROAT had gone by the morning and she
ate a hearty breakfast to make up for the tea and supper
she had missed the night before. Leaving her busy with a

paint box and several large sheets of paper, Polly went down to Maranza to see how the goat boy was progressing.

She found Gilès and the local doctor chatting together in a mixture of French and English, and it was evident from their faces that the boy was already on the way to recovery, although it would be many weeks before he could scramble over the hills with his herd again.

After saying a cordial farewell to the doctor, Giles took Polly to a café overlooking the harbor and ordered **strong black coffee,** *brioches* **and cheese.**

"Have you had any sleep, yet?" she asked.

"Yes, I snatched a couple of hours after old Charvos finally got back from helping to produce a lusty pair of twins. I'm not tired," he said.

Surprisingly, considering the physical strain of the actual rescue and the mental effort required of him later, he bore no signs of fatigue.

"You handled it terribly well," she said. "If you hadn't been there...." She let a gesture finish the sentence for her.

Giles grinned. "I suppose you've guessed what happened."

"I think so—part of it, anyway." -

He drank his coffee and ate a roll and some cheese with appetite, his expression reflective.

"It sounds crazy if you put it into words," he said presently. "Yesterday I didn't know what I wanted. Today I do. All because a silly young clot pitches over a cliff and breaks his leg. Doesn't make sense really."

"I think it does, Giles," she said gently.

He leaned across the table and put his hand over hers. "D'you know, Polly, when I looked up that cliff and saw the kid stuck in the bush, I had the most peculiar feeling. A whole lot of stuff that I'd read and never really taken in suddenly came back to me. It was as clear as if I'd had the printed page in front of me. But the strangest part was when I actually reached him. He came around for a second or two, poor little blighter, and he looked at me as if he knew that I'd probably hurt him like hell but that it couldn't be helped. Actually he's damn plucky all the way through, and he's only ten, you know. Well, it was when he opened his eyes up on the ledge that was the oddest part. I suddenly felt that this was the first time I'd ever got to grips with anything and that I had to make a go of it—that I *could* make a go of it. It doesn't sound much, I suppose but it was to me. When Charvos turned up and examined the kid and said I'd made quite a job of him, I felt as pleased as if I'd come up on the Irish Sweep.''

He broke off, reddening, slightly shamefaced. ''Sounds like a lot of sentimental hogwash, I suppose.''

Polly put her other hand over his. ''I'm so glad, Giles. I was sure you'd find it out sooner or later.'' She smiled. ''So no more beachcombing?''

He laughed. ''No more beachcombing. After the way I've slacked, I shall have to work like merry hell to catch up in fact.'' He paused, his eyes growing serious. ''One of the best things about last night was what happened just before you left. I suppose you counted on the fact that I was pretty well all in and wouldn't be likely to follow it up?''

She disengaged her hands, coloring a little. ''It seemed the only way to tell you how . . . how proud I was of you,'' she said shyly.

''I should imagine you were pretty disgusted with me after all the rot I talked the other morning on the beach.''

''No, I wasn't. I didn't really believe you.''

''Darling Polly, has anyone ever told you how sweet you are? Dozens, I suppose. Look, this calls for a celebration. Will you be free tonight? Can we paint the village red?''

''I should think so,'' she said, laughing. ''Although there's isn't much to paint or to paint it with.''

He grinned and tossed back the rest of his coffee. ''We can have a go, anyway. Romanetti's isn't quite up to the standard of the Ritz, but I'll put some pressure on him, the old robber. That's a date, then.''

IT WAS nearly midnight when Giles and Polly sauntered up the dark driveway to the castle after their celebratory dinner. Giles was now something of a hero in the village, and throughout their meal people had kept coming up to shake his hand and praise his resourcefulness and skill in rescuing the goat boy.

It was evident that he thought they were all making an unnecessary fuss about something that anyone would have tackled in similar circumstances and was considerably embarrassed at finding himself the center of attention. Indeed, on the way up the hill, he complained that their evening had been spoiled by people butting in.

Now, as they approached the castle, he said, "Grim-looking place at night, isn't it? Has it got any ghosts?"

Polly shivered and drew her cardigan closer around her shoulders. By night the castle did have a mysterious and forbidding aspect.

"Not that I know of, although Renata thinks so," she said, involuntarily drawing a little nearer to him.

He slipped his hand through the crook of her elbow. "Cold?"

"Not really. You're giving me the creeps talking about ghosts. I shall be imagining the clanking sounds in the corridors and jumping at shadows."

He laughed. "You're not the nervy type."

"I don't think one stays true to type in Corsica," she said. "Lately I've been discovering quite a number of things about myself that I hadn't noticed before."

"What kind of things?" There was an urgency in his tone.

"It's a little difficult to explain. Perhaps living in a...a dramatic country heights one's perceptions or just stimulates the imagination. Everything is a little larger than life here, isn't it?"

"I suppose it is," he agreed. "The scenery is pretty staggering, of course, but I don't know that in the long run it beats what we have at home. One can get fed up with the larger than life view, as you call it. It's all a bit like a film set, I feel."

Polly glanced up at him. "Yes, perhaps," she said nildly.

But to her there was nothing artificial about the massive peaks or the olive-clad valleys or the rocky coast lapped by a sapphire sea. That was not what she had meant at all.

Near the entrance, they stood for some moments without speaking until Giles's fingers began gently to caress her arm. She knew that he wanted to kiss her and wondered if she, too, wanted it. He took her silence and stillness for an unspoken admission that she shared his feelings and, presently, his hand moved up to her shoulder and he turned her to face him. Then with his other arm drawing her close she felt a quick pang of uncertainty and doubt, but by then it was too late to evade.

His first kiss was too brief, too hesitant, to confirm or deny anything. After an interval in which he seemed to be waiting for her to rebuff or encourage him, he kissed her again with greater confidence. When he let her go, he was breathing hard and trembling slightly.

Their embrace, Polly discovered, had not resolved anything at all. Her predominant emotion seemed to be a peculiar kind of embarrassment. And then, before she had time to collect herself, Giles seized her hands and said huskily and not very coherently, "Oh, darling, you do. . .that is. . .oh, Polly, will you marry me?"

Polly started back as if he had stung her.

"Oh, but, Giles, I don't—"

"You do care for me, don't you?" he cut in anxiously.

"Well. . .yes, of course. I've always liked you and I was glad when we met again, but—marriage! It never occurred to me."

"I don't know why not," he said with a nervous laugh. "I thought it was obvious that I was keen on you ages ago."

He attempted to draw her back into his arms, but this time Polly gently but firmly resisted and, after a second, he contented himself with kissing her hands.

"I wish now I'd told you sooner. It's been the very devil not knowing how you felt about me," he said.

"Oh, but, Giles, dear Giles—" Polly began again.

"You *do* care, don't you? You will say yes?"

She searched for words, discovering that there was no pleasure in receiving a proposal unless one was perfectly certain how to answer it.

"I don't think I can just now," she managed at last. "I'm awfully fond of you, Giles, and I . . . I respect and trust you, but marriage is such a tremendous step, so desperately important. I must think it over."

To her surprise he accepted this hesitation without protest, even as if he expected it.

"How long will you need?" he asked.

"I don't know. It's—please don't laugh at me—but it really is very sudden. We've only known each other a short time, no time at all, in fact."

He put up a hand and stroked her hair.

"Funny, I used to think love at first sight was so much claptrap," he said tenderly. "You changed my mind about that. Of course, if you do say yes I won't expect to rush you off to the nearest church. I've got to get on my feet, so we can be engaged for as long as you like." He paused, gazing at her with something close to reverence. "Don't keep me on hot bricks too long, Polly. I love you so much. I'd do anything to make you happy, I swear it."

And then, as if he could not trust himself to stay with her without seizing her in his arms again, he murmured a hoarse "Good night, my dearest," and went rushing off down the driveway.

For several minutes after he had disappeared from view, Polly stood absolutely still, her thoughts and senses in the wildest confusion. Then the rasp and flicker of a match made her jerk around with a smothered exclamation.

"Good evening," Raoul said lazily from the deep shadows shrouding the doorway. "Have a good time?"

"How long have you been there?" she demanded.

He came down the steps into the moonlight. "Some minutes."

"Do you often spy on people when they don't know you're there?" she asked scathingly.

"Not often. But your farewell was so moving that I was quite transfixed by it," he said with cool irony. "I couldn't hear what you were saying to each other but, at a guess, I'd hazard that Barrington was asking you to marry him."

Polly's cheeks burned. "Yes, if you must know, he was!" she said tartly.

"Am I to congratulate him next time we meet?"

Her hands clenched. *I must not lose my temper,* she thought grimly. *I won't lose it.*

Aloud, she said, "I'm sorry, but you'll have to contain your curiosity for a while. I haven't made up my mind, yet."

She went to stalk past him, but as she did so her cardigan, which had been draped over her shoulders, slipped off and fell on the gravel. He stooped to pick it up, but did not return it to her.

"How very English," he said derisively.

"What do you mean?"

"Marriage is not a matter to be weighed over like a business transaction, my dear," he said negligently. "Either you love him or you don't. Of course it's possible that you're too immature to recognize your emotions for what they are. But if Barrington were a Corsican he wouldn't be fool enough to give you time to consider."

"Well, he's not! And I couldn't be more glad of it!" she said sharply. "In England we don't rush into marriage and live to regret it."

She tried to retrieve the cardigan, but found that, short of engaging in an undignified tug of war, she could not.

"Slow but sure or fast and furious, the English seem to make as many mistakes as any other race," he said mildly. "There's only one sound reason for marrying a man, little one, and that's because you can't live without him."

"For a bachelor you seem to know a great deal about it," Polly retorted acidly. "You ought to write a lonely hearts column, advising people how to solve their emotional problems while standing safely in the wings yourself."

"What makes you think I'm in the wings?"

In spite of her resolve to remain calm, to deny him the satisfaction of hurting her, Polly's precarious self-control snapped.

"Because you aren't capable of any normal feelings," she said wildly. "Love is something you could never understand."

Her voice broke and no longer caring about the cardigan, she turned and fled up the steps and into the hall, running as if a demon were on her heels. When, breathless and spent, she reached the sanctuary of her room, she flung herself on the bed and buried her face in the pillow.

"I hate him! I hate him!" she whispered into the darkness. And it was then—her cheeks wet with tears of pain and rage, her slender shoulders heaving with the effort to stifle her weeping—it was then that she faced the truth. It was not hatred that racked her. For days she had been refusing to acknowledge what was really the matter with her. Sick with despair, her nails driving into her palms, she admitted the extent of her folly. She could never marry Giles because she was heart over head in love with Raoul St. Clair.

CHAPTER SIX

WHEN DAWN crept over the glassy sea, a rosy twilight
slowly burgeoning into a blaze of gold and vermilion
reflections, Polly sat at her window, already dressed,
her chin cupped in her hands. Soon, as the sun rose lazily from the horizon and the dew dried, the scent of the
maquis would be sweeter than at any other time of the
day. This morning the beauty of the scene before her
was almost unbearable, and she knew that she would
never again be free of the spell that the island had cast
over her, the island—and Raoul!

Dear God, how can I bear it, she thought, closing her
eyes against the quick hot tears that stung her lids and
smarted in her throat. Just to think of him was now a
blend of exquisite joy and intolerable pain, for, having
swept aside the last of her defenses, the love that she had
fought so desperately was no longer a secret and name-
less flicker but a fiercely burning flame. In a kind of
ecstatic agony she thought of the proud set of his dark
head, of the limber grace of his stride, of the strongly
muscled arms that had carried her up from the beach
that terrible and wonderful night when he had kissed
her, of the brilliantly blue eyes that could glitter with
contempt or light with infuriating amusement. Yet this
tide of feeling that threatened to overwhelm her was
more, far more, than a powerful physical attraction. An
attraction, however strong, could be conquered and
eventually forgotten. Love—and a love with no
future—did not die so easily.

When, sometime later, Constancia brought her morning tea, she forced herself to drink a cup and eat one of
the biscuits. And then passing the mirror on her way to
wake Marisa, she paused and looked at herself in the

glass, her lips twisting in self-derision. Men like Raoul did not fall for insignificant English girls who were not even pretty, let alone beautiful.

For the first time in her life she longed for the tantalizing loveliness that was given to some women. *But even if I did attract him,* she thought wretchedly, *there would be Antonetta to think of. She loves him, too, and she is so right for him. They have everything in common.*

"Polly? Are you awake? Is it time to get up?" A small tousled head peeped around the communicating door.

"Yes, dear, I was just coming in. What shall we do today?" Polly said briskly.

"Could we take Prunella for a picnic in the woods?"

"I should think so, if she's good. Oh, Marisa, you've had Paolo in bed with you again. He'll never learn to sleep in his box at this rate."

"He doesn't like his box. He squeaks to come in with Prunella and me," Marisa explained.

"I know, but you must be strict with him because it's healthier for animals to have their own beds, and he smells so fishy after he's had supper. Besides, when he's bigger and goes out more, his paws will be dirty, and Renata won't approve of paw prints all over the sheets. Look at him now, trying to climb up the curtain. Come here, Paolo, you little menace," Polly said, grabbing the kitten and popping him into the wastepaper basket for a few minutes while she helped Marisa to dress.

They were having breakfast when Raoul come in. At that hour he was usually out on the estate and Polly was so startled that she almost dropped the coffeepot.

"Sorry to jolt you. You dropped this somewhere," he said, putting her cardigan on a chair. "Hello, baggage. How's the menagerie today?"

"Prunella isn't very well so we're going to take her for a picnic," said Marisa. "Would you like to come with us, Uncle Raoul?"

"I would be charmed, but I'm afraid I can't," he said.

"I wish you weren't always so busy. We could have much more fun if you were with us, couldn't we, Polly?"

"You shouldn't talk with your mouth full, Marisa," Polly said, carefully peeling an orange.

Raoul laughed. "Very tactful," he said dryly. "Except for those occasional flashes of scorching candor, you're discretion personified, aren't you, Polly?"

"I try to be. Sometimes people make it very difficult," she said tightly.

"Oddly enough I think I prefer you with your hair down. But if you prefer to play the sphinx...." He shrugged, leaving the sentence unfinished. Then, tousling Marisa's hair, he went out of the room.

"Uncle Raoul is very difficult to understand sometimes, isn't he?" Marisa said seriously.

Impossible, Polly thought crossly. Aloud, she said, "He just has a peculiar sense of humor, Marisa. Shall we share this orange or would you rather have a banana?"

She did not see Giles again for two days, and then on the third afternoon, he came up the drive while she was drowsing on the lawn.

"It's all right for me to come calling, I hope," he said, dropping onto the grass beside her chair and waving to Marisa, who was bandaging her doll some distance away.

Polly laid aside the flounced cotton petticoat she was mending and smoothed her hair. She had been half-asleep, nodding over her work, and did not feel at all in the mood to cope with the subject Giles probably intended to broach.

"Why not?" she said with a smile.

"I spent the whole of yesterday climbing. I nearly lost myself and had to spend the night in the open," he said. "Not that it would have done me much harm, but I imagine it's a bit eerie up in some of those gorges after dark."

"Ought you to climb by yourself? Supposing you had an accident like the goat boy."

"Oh, there's not much risk if one doesn't tackle the tougher faces, and I've been at it since I was quite a kid," he assured her. "What have you been up to?"

"Nothing special, I'm getting lazy."

He plucked a blade of grass and split it into two. "You haven't been thinking about what I asked you the other night, I suppose?"

Polly hesitated, wishing she need not hurt him but knowing that to prevaricate would only cause him more pain in the end.

"Yes, I have," she said in a low voice.

He did not look at her. "And?"

"I'm sorry, Giles, I can't marry you," she said unhappily.

He was silent for a long time, and Polly was torn between trying to soften her refusal and fear of making it harder.

After a while he felt for his pipe and filled it. "Thanks for giving it to me straight."

She fidgeted with her thimble. "I feel a horror. I wish now that we'd never met. You've been so nice to me."

"You can't help it, sweetie," he said with a wry glance. "One falls or one doesn't. Unfortunately it's one sphere where the old 'look before you leap' adage doesn't apply. One doesn't realize one's leaped until one lands. I'm not the first chap to land headfirst. I take it that it's just that you don't feel the vital spark. There's no other reason, is there?"

"No, there's no other reason." She hesitated again. "I suppose you'll be leaving Maranza now?"

"Not unless you want me out of the way. Don't worry, I won't try plaguing you into anything. I just have an odd feeling that I might come in handy." Seeing the anxiety in her eyes, he added, "I won't be washed up in the bay tomorrow morning, if that's what you're thinking."

Polly shivered. "Don't joke about it, Giles. People do rash things if they're unhappy."

"Not me. I don't pretend that I'll be in top form right away, but I'm not the type to feel my whole life is

washed up because you can't say 'yes.'" He paused,
then added gruffly, "If a chap really loves a girl he
doesn't throw the guilt for his sticky end in her lap." He
got to his feet and looked down at her. "Don't look so
upset. I'll get over it. And remember, if there's anything
I can do—I can't think what exactly, but something
might crop up—I'll be at the usual place. 'Bye."

And, with a smile that did not reach his eyes, he went
off by the way he had come. Polly watched him until he
disappeared from sight, her heart heavy. Men had one
great advantage, she thought. They could at least
declare their feelings. For women love had to be a secret
burden.

TWO DAYS LATER, during lunch, Raoul said. "I'm going
over to Porto tomorrow. It will be a good opportunity
to show you Les Calanches."

"Les Calanches?" Polly said interrogatively.

"It's a rather spectacular stretch of coast just north
of a little place called Piana." He looked at Marisa.
"I'm afraid you can't come with us this time, baggage.
We may be late back and it will be too long a day for
you."

Marisa looked disappointed but accepted the decision
uncomplainingly. One of her most appealing qualities
was that she never grizzled or sulked when told she
could not have or do something.

So, a little after nine the next day, Polly climbed into
the jeep with the picnic lunch that Renata had prepared
and, waving goodbye to Marisa and Constancia, they
drove away. Earlier that morning Polly had not been
sure whether she wanted to spend a day alone with
Raoul, but as they swung out of the gates and turned
north, her spirits lifted and she determined to enjoy
herself.

They reached Piana, a village of rose-colored stone
houses with a magnificent view of the deep green gulf of
Porto, at midmorning, and drove straight through it.
And then accustomed to the scenic beauty of the island,
but unprepared for the most amazing of all natural

wonders, Polly saw the red rocks of the Calanches. It was the most fantastically beautiful spectacle she had ever seen. On either side of the narrow roadway, extending for about a mile, the landscape was strewn with massive porphyry rocks of every roseate hue from softest pink to vivid carmine. But it was not only the amazing colors of the rocks that astonished her, but their strange and often grotesque forms. Some were reminiscent of Epstein sculptures, other reminded her of the leering gargoyles she had seen on the towers of Notre Dame Cathedral in Paris.

"This really isn't the best time of day to see it," Raoul said, stopping the jeep. "Just about sunset when the shadows are beginning to fall is the perfect moment. People either think they're in Heaven or Hell."

They left the jeep and walked for a little distance while he pointed out the rocks that were so realistic that they had been given names—the Calf's Head, the Bishop and the President that, he told her, bore a remarkable likeness to a former French president.

When after half an hour of scrambling around they drove on, Raoul explained that their destination was actually some way beyond Porto.

"I'm going to see an old lady who used to be my mother's nurse," he said. "She's quite a character and remarkably spry considering she's well over ninety. I visit her four or five times a year. She likes to ramble about old times, although of course most of the events she remembers happened long before I was born."

"What's her name?" Polly asked.

"Sophia Bonelli. It's a pity she can't speak English. She could tell you everything you wanted to know about vendettas. Her uncle, Antoine, was one of the island's most famous bandits."

"What did he do?"

"He was in love with the sister of the mayor of his village. The mayor didn't approve of him as a brother-in-law, so he forbade the wedding and tried to confiscate the Bonelli land. Antoine shot him and took to the *maquis*. Then he fell for another girl who was already engaged. Soon after she'd been married to her fiancé, he shot him, also. There were quite a few more killings and then the police tried to storm the hideout that he and his brother had at a place called Pentica.''

''Did they kill them?''

''No, they failed and lost several men in the attempt. Eventually it got to the point when the French minister of war ordered an armed expedition to capture them. That also failed because Antoine was very popular in the district and the people helped him to make a getaway.''

''So what happened in the end?''

''Well, his brother, who was a really bad lot, was an outlaw for the rest of his life, but Antoine ended up as a forest guide over at Vizzavona. He died at a ripe old age some years before the first war. Sophia remembers him quite clearly. He was an enormous man even when he was old, and she told me he used to wear a woolen sock on his head and smoke a long pipe. I expect Renata's often told Marisa about him. He's a kind of Corsican Robin Hood.'' He turned his head and smiled at her. ''I used to play at being Antoine Bonelli when I was a kid.'' Then he asked, ''Feeling hungry?''

''Yes, I am a little.''

''Right. We'll stop about half a mile ahead in the chestnut forest.''

After a lunch of sandwiches, fruit and hot coffee from a vacuum flask, Raoul suggested that they would walk in the forest for half an hour. Sophia would sleep after her own midday meal and would not welcome visitors until a little later in the day, he explained.

It was pleasantly cool and very quiet under the trees, and Polly hummed softly to herself as they strolled through the green dimness that was lit here and there by pools of sunlight that had found a gap in the thick tracery of branches.

''You know, you are one of the very few women who can wear trousers attractively,'' Raoul said suddenly from behind her. ''Or has Barrington already told you that?''

She paused to pluck a spray of leaves from a bush and examined them as if they were a rare botanical specimen of consuming interest.

"Giles never makes such personal remarks," she said coolly.

"Why? Isn't it 'done' in England?" he inquired teasingly.

"That depends. Not by employers to employees."

"But our relationship is not primarily that of employer and employee, is it?"

She was surprised into giving him a quick uncertain glance. "What do you mean?"

He dropped onto a patch of moss and leaned against a tree trunk. "If we're going to discuss that, we might as well relax."

Polly sat down near, but not too near to him. The trousers to which he had referred were tapered slacks of dark blue linen, and with them she wore a lighter blue shirt with a yellow cotton kerchief knotted around her throat. Now, feeling the noon heat even under the shelter of the chestnuts and pines, she unfastened this and pushed it into her pocket.

"Do you really think of me primarily as an employer?" Raoul asked lighting a cigarette and lounging with one knee raised.

"Well. . . naturally!"

"On the contrary, it's most unnatural. No, don't jump down my throat again. I'm not calling you a liar. No doubt you really believe it—that just goes to show how extraordinarily innocent you are."

Polly sat cross-legged, fiddling with the cords of her espadrilles.

"I suppose you find that very amusing," she said coldly.

"No, I think it could be extremely dangerous. People who haven't yet discovered, or who refuse to face, the fundamental principles of human relationships can make life devilishly awkward for themselves and everybody concerned with them."

"And how exactly am I doing that?"

"You aren't—yet. But I suspect that you will sooner or later."

"I really don't see what all this has to do with the fact that Giles doesn't make personal remarks."

He was silent for a few minutes, smoking contemplatively. "No doubt he'd like to, but isn't sure how you might take them."

"A scruple that obviously doesn't afflict you," she returned crisply.

He laughed. "You'll have to hit harder than that to draw blood, my dear."

"Could I?"

"Probably not, I have a fairly thick skin. I suppose you prefer the sensitive type."

"I certainly don't think it's admirable to be callous and unfeeling," she retorted with some heat.

He slid down onto his back and burying the cigarette in the moss, locked his hands under his head and looked up at the gnarled branches.

"You're not very consistent, are you?" he said mildly. "You disapprove of my paying you a compliment because I also pay you wages, but you don't hesitate to give me a very candid reading of my character."

"I...I didn't mean that personally," she said quickly. "I just meant that I prefer sensitive people to...to hard ones."

"Oh, I see." His smile was sardonic.

She hesitated, remembering the much more scathing opinions she had flung at him on the night of Giles's proposal.

"I never mean to be rude...and unkind," she said uncomfortably. "But you have a way of saying things that's sometimes hard to take. The other night, for instance—"

"Ah, yes, the other night was a notable instance," he said dryly. Then watching her under half-closed lids, "Are you nerving yourself to tell me that you might have exaggerated my barbarity a trifle?"

"I shouldn't have said what I did."

"Why? Because you're my employee?"

"Not only that, it was one of the stupid things one does say when one loses one's temper."

"If it will relieve your conscience, I didn't take it too seriously. By the way, have you put Barrington out of his misery yet?"

Her fingers tightened on her ankles, but she met his glance steadily.

"Yes. . . I have," she said quietly.

He held her eyes for a long moment, and then with a single lithe movement he got to his feet. "It's time we were moving on," he said briskly.

The rest of the journey passed in silence until, a mile or so beyond a straggling hamlet, they came to a steep and twisting track that led up to a small stone cottage.

"That's old Sophia's lair," Raoul said briefly. "You'd better grab a handhold. The track is pretty rough."

As they came up to the cottage, a middle-aged woman came out of the door, and greeted Raoul with great cordiality. They chatted for some minutes and then he introduced Polly to her.

"She's a granddaughter who comes up from the village every day. Sophia refuses to live with any of her family. Her husband built this place for her seventy years ago and she is determined to die here," he explained.

Polly held out her hand, and the woman dipped in a form of curtsey and clasped it with her own toil-worn calloused fingers. Then she unhitched a mule from a post near the door and bade them goodbye.

At first, after the blazing sunlight outside, the interior of the cottage seemed so dark that Polly could see nothing. But presently she saw the old nurse was lying on a rough palliasse in one corner, her bent shoulders propped up by a mountain of soiled pillows. For some minutes she was too occupied in exploring the basket of provisions that Raoul had brought her to notice that he had also brought a visitor. Then he said something to her, and she peered at Polly with beady eyes that were like two black buttons amid a maze of wrinkles and seams.

"Come a bit closer. Her eyesight is not too good," he said, opening wooden shutters in the wall behind the bed and letting in more light.

Shyly, a little fearful that the old lady might take a dislike to her, Polly drew nearer the bed and smiled at the ancient, withered face with its frame of wispy white hair. Presently a clawlike hand stretched out and fastened on her wrist, and she found herself being pulled down onto the bed with a strength that was quite astonishing in someone so aged. In a voice that alternated between a hoarse whisper and a suddenly raucous cackle the old woman spoke to Raoul.

"What does she say?" Polly asked curiously.

"That in Corsica women have never needed to put red dye on their lips to make men want to kiss them, and that my father never told her that in his country women wore trousers," he said, looking amused.

Polly blushed, and this seemed to amuse Sophia, for she burst into a hoarse rattle of laughter and patted the girl's arm.

"She says that in spite of the trousers you are a pretty little bird," Raoul translated.

He spoke to the old lady and hearing Marisa's name Polly guessed that he was explaining her function at the castle.

When he had finished Sophia replied at some length.

"She says that a healthy girl should be caring for her own children, not other people's," he said. "She wants to know if all the young men have left England, otherwise why is a girl of your age unmarried? She was married at fifteen and had three children by the time she was twenty. She—"

He broke off as Sophia began to speak again, and although he laughed and made some amusing reply, he did not translate whatever other comments she had made.

"Wouldn't you like to talk privately?" Polly said. "Shall I have a look around outside?"

"Do you mind?"

"No, of course not." With a smile at the old lady, she rose from the bed and slipped outside.

Leaning against the hood of the jeep, her eyes scanning the vista of mountains and gorges across the valley, she thought that in some respects Raoul was extraordinarily nice. Not many men in his position would take the trouble to visit a wizened old crone in a broken-down and rather dirty hovel just because she had served a previous generation of St. Clairs. Always immaculate himself, he gave no sign that the old woman's grimy bedding and greasy shawl offended him.

She wondered what Sophia had been like as a girl. It seemed impossible that those puckered toothless lips had ever been ripely red or the sparse, white hair veiling the dry scalp had once fallen in thick dark tresses on smoothly rounded shoulders.

How strange to live for ninety years and outlast all the people you once knew, Polly thought. But perhaps for Sophia the passage of the years had been less ruthless than for people in other countries. Her world had not changed much.

Men still straddled their mules soon after dawn and rode off into the hills, returning at dusk with vast loads of brushwood piled behind them. Women still baked their bread in a communal oven and beat their washing on smooth stones at the edge of the stream.

Presently Raoul put his head out of the door and said, "Come and have a glass of wine. Sophia wants to read your hand."

As Polly reentered the cottage, he added, "Her family believe she has the gift of seeing into the future, but don't let her do it if you're going to take it too seriously."

"I don't mind. I love having my fortune told. I've an aunt who reads teacups, but her forecasts have never come true, yet," she said with a smile.

When they had each drunk a glass of wine, Sophia took both Polly's hands in hers and bent over them, muttering to herself. She studied them for so long that

Polly began to wonder if, like many old people, she had suddenly dropped off to sleep. But at last she released her hold and lay back against the pillows. Then in a strange chanting tone she began to talk.

"It sounds as if she was reading my past, present and future," Polly said when the prognosis concluded, Sophia indicated that she would like another glass of wine. "Oh, do tell me what she saw. Was it good or bad?"

Raoul poured out the wine. "I'm not sure. She always uses very picturesque metaphors in these matters, probably to make them sound more impressive. I'm afraid it didn't sound too promising."

"I don't mind. What did she say?" Polly persisted.

"Are you sure you won't brood over it?"

"No, of course not, do tell me."

He shrugged. "All right. First of all she said that the head of your family was a wise and good man and that your mother had been fortunate in bearing him many sons."

"But that's extraordinary," Polly exclaimed. "How could she possibly know about the boys? You didn't mention them, did you?"

He shook his head and smiled. "There's a lot of luck involved in fortune-telling, you know."

"And then?" Polly urged eagerly.

"Then she said that although many men had asked your father for permission to court you, none had touched your heart." He grinned. "I don't know whether they asked permission, but I daresay the gist of it is true."

Polly colored slightly and then a frightful possibility occurring to her turned crimson. Supposing Sophia really could read the future, and part of the present? Supposing she knew who *had* touched Polly's heart?

"I'm not sure that I do want to hear it after all," she said hurriedly.

"Oh come, a minute ago you were all ears," Raoul said mildly. Then he said, a glint in his eyes, "She hasn't discovered any deep dark secrets as far as I can tell."

"I haven't any, so she couldn't."

"Do you want me to go on or not?"

"Well. . .all right."

"She said there was a man who would change your life. Incidentally, I didn't gather when he was actually on the scene or was still hovering some way ahead. Anyway, according to her, you would turn your face from him but might regret it later. Then your life that had always been calm would become a great torrent and you would have to struggle for many days before being carried into still waters again."

"Is that all?"

"Just about. She did add that you would probably have three children, the first one a boy."

Polly avoided his eyes. "I don't know about this man or the great torrent, but I hope she's right about the children," she said as casually as she could manage. "Will you thank her for me, please?"

Raoul did so, and the rest of their visit passed in a two-sided conversation about the past. Then, when it became apparent that the old woman was tiring, they said goodbye and went down to the village to the granddaughter's house where Polly spent more than an hour playing with an adorably pudgy infant wearing nothing but a shrunken vest, and Raoul conversed with the older members of the family. Later they were offered and accepted a light meal, after which Raoul asked if she minded if he left her for half an hour to call on the head man of the community. In fact his call lasted for nearly two hours, but although no could speak English she found it was not difficult to communicate with them by signs and nods. When Raoul came back she was intimating a group of children into the art of hopscotch and said smilingly that there was no need for him to apologize as she had been enjoying herself.

The sun was sinking behind the mountains and the sky was streaked with mother of pearl and gold when they started for home, not by the way they had come, by a more inland route. As they drove away Polly turned in her seat for a last glimpse of the village. Without knowing it she heaved a long sigh.

"I'm afraid it wasn't very entertaining for you," Raoul said, seeing her rather forlorn expression.

"But it was, I enjoyed it." She paused and then said diffidently, "I was just thinking of all the places one goes to for a short time and never revisits."

"I expect you'll come up here, again."

"I may not be at Maranza next time you visit Sophia."

"Thinking of leaving us?"

"No, not at the moment—but I can't stay forever."

"Who knows? You wouldn't be the first to lose your heart to Corsica." He took one hand off the wheel and felt for his cigarettes. "Sorry, I forgot. You've already given it to Barrington, haven't you?"

Polly looked away from him and said nothing.

"Still not a hundred percent sure?" he asked. "He has more patience with you than I would."

A strand of hair blew across her cheek and she brushed it back.

"You told me the other night that you wouldn't give a woman time to make up her mind," she said carefully. "What could you do about it?"

He laughed. "There are methods of speeding the process."

Her lips were dry and she ran the tip of her tongue over them. "What . . . what sort of methods?"

"With a girl like you?"

Her fingers, resting on the rim of the door, tightened. "With anyone."

"One can't generalize. One suits one's tactics to the person concerned. Shall I assume for the sake of discussion that you're the objective?"

Her throat was tight. "All right. Me," she said recklessly.

"It would be simple enough," he said casually. "I would choose a suitable setting, make sure that there were no untimely interruptions, and make love to you. If after five minutes or so you weren't prepared to follow me through fire and water, it would be obvious to both of us that whatever else we might have in common, the essential element was lacking.''

"Whereupon you would wave me—the girl in the case—goodbye and look around for someone else, I suppose?'' she said tonelessly.

"Very probably. It's no use trying to start a fire without kindling." He paused. "I hope Barrington knows that.''

"Why are you so against Giles? What's the matter with him?''

"Nothing at all, he seems a very decent lad. I just don't think he's right for you.''

She made a restive movement. "I don't want to talk about it anymore.''

He smiled at her. "Whatever you say.''

Soon it was dark and watching the long beam of the headlights probe the way before them, Polly found her eyelids beginning to flicker. She was half-asleep when she heard Raoul swear and hurriedly sat upright.

"What's the matter?''

He did not have to answer. Even as she spoke she heard the engine misfiring. A few moments later they were at a standstill.

"Hell! This is all we need," Raoul said sharply.

"Have we run out of gas?''

He shook his head and peering at the gauge she saw that the tank was nearly half-full.

"Hang on, I'll take a look.''

Producing a flashlight he climbed out and lifted the hood. Almost immediately she heard him clip off another curse.

"The ignition has burned out," he said, straightening.

"Can you mend it?''

He slammed the hood back into place and came to the offside door.

"No, it's a garage job. I'm afraid we've had it.''

"Perhaps there'll be another car along presently and we can get a tow.''

"Not on this road, we're probably the first vehicle to come over the pass all day."

"How far are we from home? Can't we walk the rest of the way?"

."I might, but you couldn't. It's a good twenty miles."

She was silent for some moments. Then she said, "Well, there must be a village quite close. They'd put us up if we explained, wouldn't they?"

"Yes, if we could get there before the early hours. I'm sorry about this but it couldn't have happened in a worse spot. The nearest holding is six miles across country, and with the best will in the world you'd never make it. By road it's more like ten."

Polly swallowed. She was tired and hungry again and ten miles of walking in the dark was a formidable distance.

"What are we going to do, then?" she asked helplessly.

"There's only one thing we can do," he said tersely. "Stick it out until morning. I'm sorry, but it's just one of those things."

CHAPTER SEVEN

"YOU MEAN, stay in the jeep all night?" she said blankly.

"Not if we can find somewhere more comfortable. There's an old watchtower on the other side of the ridge that might be reasonably habitable. I'll take a look at it. I won't be more than half an hour."

"Oh, please—can't I come with you?"

He was silent for a moment. "It may be too rat ridden to sleep in. You'd be better off waiting here until I've reconnoitered. There's nothing to be scared of."

"I'm not scared," she said quickly, a shade too quickly. "I'd just rather go."

"As you please." He offered a hand to help her down, but she managed unaided. "It's a good thing you're wearing slacks. The track up there, if there's anything left of it now, will be pretty overgrown. If you're coming I may as well take what gear we've got. It will save a second trip if the place is habitable."

Polly waited while he collected a groundsheet and knapsack from the back of the jeep and then, in silence, they set off down the road.

"You'd better take my hand," he said, after they had gone about ten yards. "It's easy to sprain an ankle on these ruts and I want to save the flashlight as much as possible. We might need it more later on."

"I can see my way all right."

"Famous last words." He reached out and caught her wrist, drawing her nearer to him. Then his fingers slipped down and closed firmly over hers. "This is no time for a show of feminist independence."

Polly did not answer. She concentrated on avoiding the roughest places, determinedly ignoring the fact that her pulse had quickened. She was glad when he slowed

down, flicked on the flashlight and began to probe the
scrub along the roadside for some sign of an entry. Presently the narrow beam illuminated a massive boulder.

"Ah, here it is," Raoul said. "Hang onto the groundsheet, will you? By the look of it, I'll need both arms
free to clear a way."

He hitched the knapsack over both shoulders, hooked
the flashlight onto the front of his belt and plunged into
the bushes. As he had forecast, the way up to the tower
was now almost completely obscured by heather and
creeping plants, but here and there a narrow ribbon of
pebbly sand was still visible. In places the slope was steep
enough for her to welcome a pull up and halfway up she
felt a tug on the back of her shirt and stopped short too
late to prevent a long bramble from rending the fabric.

"All in one piece?" Raoul asked, when they reached
the summit of the ridge.

"I think so."

"Good girl." He turned away to look toward the tower that was surrounded by an expanse of turf. "Doesn't
look too inviting, does it? Come on, let's investigate."

The tower was about thirty feet tall, and originally a
spiral stairway had led to the top, but time and weather
had crumbled away the greater part of this and ivy obscured most of what was left. There was still a wooden
door barring the arched entrance, and Raoul kicked it
open and shone the flashlight into the blackness within.

"Hm, seems quite homely," he said, going in.

Polly hesitated, half expecting a cloud of bats to beat
angrily out or to hear a muffled moan, but when nothing happened she followed him inside and saw that
although the flashlight showed thick draperies of cob-
web in the angle of the low ceiling, there was nothing
particularly sinister about the interior. There seemed to
be no means of access to the upper apartment.

"What do you think? Shall we make the best of this
or go back to the jeep?" Raoul asked. "At least there's
a bit more leg room here, and with a pile of heather and
the groundsheet you wouldn't be too uncomfortable."

"Yes, all right, as you say, there's more room."

"Right. We haven't got much in the way of food, I'm afraid, but at least we can have a cup of coffee. I'll get a fire going outside."

"But we haven't got any water."

"There's a spring not far away."

"Have you stayed up here before, then?"

He shrugged off the knapsack and put it on the ground. "Yes, I used to camp here as a boy. You put our sandwich wrappings back in the knapsack, didn't you? They'll do to get the fire going."

Ten minutes later the glow of the flames lit the face of the tower and the pleasant smell of wood smoke drifted on the air.

"Do you want to come to the spring with me or will you stay here?" he asked.

"I'll stay here and watch the fire."

He looked at her and she knew he was not deceived.

"I'll be within call," he said.

While he was gone she fed some more sticks to the flames and tried not to imagine that dark shapes lurked in the bushes. He was back within ten minutes.

Soon the can full of water he had fetched was heating over the fire. While they were waiting for it to boil, he set about collecting armfuls of heather and arranging it in two mounds on either side of the room.

"This won't be as soft as your usual mattress and you'll probably find a beetle or two making friends with you, but at least you won't wake up tomorrow with a permanent crick in your back," he said.

"What about you?" Polly asked, as he spread the groundsheet over the shorter of the mounds.

"I've slept rough before and I don't scratch so easily."

Although they had no milk or sugar left, the coffee tasted surprisingly good, and Raoul divided the remaining ham sandwich and four biscuits between them.

"Want to try a cigarette to stave off the pangs?" he asked, when they had eaten these meager provisions.

Polly shook her head and watched him light up and lean back on one elbow.

"At least you won't be stumped for news when next

you write home," he said with a grin. "Were you ever a Girl Guide, or is all this completely new to you?"

"Yes, I was a guide for a while—but our camps were nothing like this. It was all very organized and much the same as being at home except for the tents and the rather terrible food we cooked."

"I'm sure you learned any number of useful knots," he said with a twinkle.

She laughed. Their predicament was proving much easier than she had expected, mainly because he seemed to regard it as a fairly common mishap.

"Won't they be dreadfully worried at the castle when we don't turn up?" she asked.

"They'll probably have a good idea of what's happened."

She drew up her knees and clasped her arms around them, watching the sticks glow white and then fall into ash in the heart of the fire. Suddenly she was happier than ever before. For a few hours she would be alone with him here on the mountainside. For a few hours, because he thought the breakdown had upset her, he would be gentle and companionable.

Then with a pang of guilt she remembered Antonetta, remembered that she had no right to be glad that they were here. Unconsciously her brows puckered and she bit her lip.

"Don't look so worried. You aren't hopelessly compromised. Our roads being what they are this sort of situation isn't particularly unusual," he said.

The bantering tone stung her. She had thought that, for once, he would be kind.

"That hadn't even occurred to me," she said, with a cool glance. "Anyway, I've been compromised, as you call it, already."

His brows arched and then he grinned. "Ah, yes, your trip on the *Corsair*. But you weren't alone with me then, were you?"

"I don't suppose your crew would have helped me if you'd...." She stopped short. After a minute, she said,

"Won't someone see the fire and wonder who is up here?"

"I doubt it. If they do, they're not likely to investigate. In this country it's wiser to mind one's own business."

"What do you mean?"

He shrugged. "Certain members of the community don't care to have their privacy disturbed."

Her eyes widened. "You mean—bandits? But I thought they were a thing of the past. Surely the police—"

"Let sleeping dogs lie—unless they're forced to take action," he said casually. "What's the matter? Don't you think I'm capable of protecting you from any unfriendly visitors?"

"Yes, of course," she said hurriedly.

"Even if you were alone, you'd be perfectly safe. Bandit isn't synonymous with ruffian in our language. It merely signifies someone who has been obliged to take to the hills for the time being."

"But surely if they have to do that they must have done something criminal."

"Yes—according to British or French laws, although it isn't always so. Some men go into hiding for quite trifling offenses. They haven't too much confidence in foreign justice and, to a Corsican, three months in the *maquis* is preferable to three weeks, even three days, in jail. We have a deep-rooted antipathy for being locked up, you see."

He ground out his cigarette on a stone and got to his feet. "The going to the spring isn't as rough as the way up here. Would you like a wash before you turn in? I've got a clean handkerchief you can dry on."

The water in the small pool to which he took her was icy but refreshing. It emerged from a natural culvert higher up and fell in a series of miniature waterfalls for several miles, Raoul told her. Polly cupped her hands and drank some. Then she rinsed her face and arms and dried them on the handkerchief he gave her.

"It won't be much use to you now," she said apologetically, handing it back.

"I'll dry by the fire."

On the way back to the tower she got a small but sharp pebble in her sandal and had to stop to shake it out. As she wobbled on one foot, he slipped a hand under her arm to steady her. His fingers were cold from the water, but they seemed to burn through the thin cotton of her sleeve. Her heart began to pound and she stammered over her thanks. As they moved on she was acutely aware of his tall figure just behind her.

The fire was burning low when they reached it. Raoul threw some more sticks onto it and Polly felt for her pocket comb and began to tug at the tangles that the breeze had made in her hair. She had not spoken since they left the pool and she was afraid of stammering again. She was beginning to tremble and every nerve in her body was taut.

"My God! Do you have to make it so obvious!" he snapped harshly.

She stared at him, shrinking from the anger on his face.

"If I'd known you'd be like this about it I'd have walked it."

"I . . . I don't know w-what you mean."

His nostrils flared and she saw a pulse beating at his temple.

"D'you think I'm such a monster that I'd have to maroon us both in the middle of nowhere before I'd have the guts to make love to you?" he said brutally. "D'you think I don't know that you've been scared out of your wits ever since the damned jeep stopped; that you've been waiting like a hypnotized rabbit for me to pounce?"

Polly tried to protest, to explain, to tell him that he was wrong, cruelly and hatefully wrong, but no words came. She could only stand there, shivering, paralyzed by the searing contempt on his face.

"All right, if that's what you're cringing about, I'll prove your point." In one stride he was beside her, his fingers biting into her shoulders. "It's about time you had some justification for all those attractive adjectives ou've flung at me," he said between set teeth.

The next instant she was locked in his arms and he was kissing her eyes and her cheeks and her throat. For a second the touch of his lips was a bliss that she had no will to resist, and then she began to struggle, pitting her full strength against the steel-hard arms enclosing her. Her efforts were futile. With a savage laugh he pinioned her against him with one arm and thrust his other hand into her hair. Then forcing her head back he pressed his mouth on hers.

When at last he let her go she almost fell. For perhaps ten seconds he stared at her, a look on his face that she had never seen before. Then without a word he kicked out the fire and disappeared into the dimness.

WHEN POLLY woke up, the sun was pouring through the open doorway. Turning her head, she looked toward the other bed. It was empty: it had not been slept on at all. Rubbing her eyes she sat up and listened for sounds of activity outside. Only the murmur of bees and the rustle of the breeze in the bushes stirred the stillness. She looked at her watch. It was quarter-past seven. The she noticed that a piece of paper weighted with a stone was on the beaten earth floor beside her couch. The note, written with a stub of pencil on a scrap of sandwich paper, was barely legible, but after some seconds she deciphered it as, "Gone to village. Back around eight. Stay put. R."

A faint smile curved her mouth. *Stay put*. What else did he expect? That she would try to make her own way home on foot with no inkling where she was now, let alone the direction of Maranza?

Getting to her feet she unbuttoned her shirt and shook it out, tracking down some particles of heather and an agitated ant that had found their way into her underclothes during the night.

Puzzled, she discovered that there were bruises on both her arms, faint darkish marks midway between shoulder and elbow. Then she remembered the violence with which he had grabbed her and hauled her against him. Her face and throat flamed.

The prospect of waiting around for three-quarters of an hour, perhaps longer, with nothing to do but think was unattractive. She decided to go over to the pool and wash. As she went outside she noticed that another scrap of paper had been fastened to the door with a rusty nail. On it was a rough drawing of a clenched fist holding some kind of flower that she would not have recognized as a lily had she not already seen the same device in the central pane of one of the stained glass windows lighting the hall of Castel Maranza. She had assumed than that it had some kind of armorial significance, but was mystified as to its purpose here, scrawled on a piece of paper on the door of the tower.

The little brook sparkled and bubbled in the sun and the pool in the rocks reflected the blue sky and small cotton-wool clouds that drifted lazily across it. Kneeling beside it, she held back her hair and dipped her face under the flowing surface. When she sat back on her heels a small gray green lizard was watching her from a crevice, alert to scuttle out of sight, its tiny throat pulsing. Watching it, she thought of dinosaurs and pterodactyls and reflected that the interior of Corsica with its deep forests and gaunt rock forms was probably little changed from the days when weird primeval creatures roamed the mountain sides and deep, isolated valleys. In England there were few tracts of countryside still untouched by civilization: few places where one could walk for miles without coming across a railway or a road or having the illusion of being alone with nature broken by the sight of a distant radar mast. Here, one could dream oneself back in the Stone Age and forget that little more than a hundred miles to the northwest, on the Côte d'Azur, the money-made giants of the twentieth century lay snoring in air-conditioned suites where the flowers were waxy hot-house blooms with wired stems and the water was made tasteless by chemical purifiers.

Leaving the lizard to bask undisturbed, she walked slowly back to the tower. Combing her hair, applying lipstick, dusting down her slacks, she put off the moment when she would have to think of Raoul. But presently there was nothing more to be done than to sit on the turf with her back against a sun-warmed boulder and consider the man whose every word and action made him a greater enigma.

She wondered where he had slept, if he had slept. Strangely, she herself had fallen asleep almost at once and rested soundly and dreamlessly until the sunlight had roused her half an hour ago. Why had his belief that she was afraid made him so angry? And why had he looked at her so strangely before stamping out the embers of the fire and disappearing into the night? The memory of that final bruising kiss sent a tremor down her spine. The night that Giles had asked her to marry him, she had told Raoul that he was incapable of any normal feelings. Now, with mingled humiliation and regret, she knew how wrong she had been. That air of cool indifference that had so often infuriated her, the negligent amusement with which he parried any attempts to rile him, were only masks. Beneath the veneer of impassivity lay all the fire and turbulence of his island forebears; the hot blood and savage temper that, though leashed and disciplined, were as much part of his heritage as the castle on the cliffs and the emerald sea and the scent of the *maquis*.

Examining her own reactions she found that although those fierce kisses, devoid of all tenderness, had been a harsh blow to her pride, regret was stronger than chagrin. With a wash of shame she knew that her struggle to break free had been prompted, not by genuine revulsion, but by the most shoddy kind of moral cowardice.

All the time she had been straining against his iron grip in a hopeless attempt to avert her face, a part of her had wanted to surrender to his strength, to fling her arms around his neck and yield to his kisses. Now, her face buried against her updrawn knees, her heart pounding, she knew that it was not Raoul whom she despised, but herself. *Oh, why am I being such a fool,* she thought bitterly. *Even if, by some miracle, he did*

*love me, he'd make an impossible husband. No, he
wouldn't,* whispered the small treacherous voice inside
her. *You could manage him. That's why you love him—
just because he is arrogant and overbearing and lord of
all he surveys. And that's why you don't love Giles—
because he'd always let you have your own way, because
he'd put you on a pedestal and never realize that women
don't want to be worshipped like goddesses.*

Suddenly, in the curious way that the mind somtimes
produces a seeming irrelevant vision of some past incident, Polly remembered a spirited argument that she
had had with a friend of her brother Nick's several years
before. She had been very young at the time and more
opinionated than she was now, and the young man had
had a patronizing, worldly manner that had irritated her
because he was only a year or so her senior and not specially bright. Somehow the conversation had touched on
suffragettes, and Tony or Toby, or whatever his name
had been, had said that all the palaver over women's
right to the franchise had been a waste of time, just as
sending girls to university was a waste of money. Girls,
he had declared grandly, only took up careers to give
them a better chance of hooking some poor unsuspect-
ing male as a husband, and later they were too busy
washing diapers and gossiping over the fence to take an
intelligent interest in government and world affairs that,
in any event, were too deep for them.

Partly because he was a very good-looking boy and
knew it, and partly because she knew that his arbitrary
views had an element of truth, she had counterattacked
with fierce resentment. Now, remembering her passionate defense of her sex that had ended with the defiant statement that she would never marry a man who
held similar views, she smiled to herself. There would always be a few women for whom making a home and rearing children was not enough, but for herself and millions
of others, a husband and family and the placid routine
of cleaning and cooking and offering love and comfort
was the best life had to offer. The trouble was that for
her, there would only ever be one man, and because

he was unattainable her dreams were only dreams empty of hope.

It was a few minutes to eight when she heard voices carrying up the hillside and, climbing onto a rock that overlooked the valley, saw Raoul returning. He was leading a mule and was accompanied by a small ragged boy of about Marisa's age. As she watched, he looked upward, saw her and raised a hand. It was some minutes before the little party reached the clearing around the tower: Raoul looking normal, the mule snorting irritably and the boy puffing.

"Been up long?" Raoul asked, hitching the mule to a sapling.

Polly crimsoned. "About an hour. What is the mule for?"

"For you to ride. Six miles is a goodish walk without a proper breakfast. Fortunately one of the village families has a grandson visiting them from Calvi and he has a motorbike. It's a pretty ancient contraption, but it should get us back to Maranza in reasonable time."

His tone was so ordinary, his whole manner so commonplace, that she could almost believe that the events of last night had never happened.

"What about the jeep?" she asked, trying to match his ease.

"I've made arrangements for it to be fixed later. Here, I've brought you some bread and cheese and the boy has a bottle of wine if you're thirsty."

He handed her a package containing a hefty sandwich of crusty bread and pungent Broccio cheese, then spoke to the boy who produced a bottle from his patched hand-me-down vest.

Polly smiled at him and received a shy beam in return. "What's his name?" she asked.

"Tino. I wouldn't get too friendly if I were you. He's a dirty little scoundrel."

"Oughtn't he to ride the mule? Twelve miles is much too far for the child to walk."

"He's tougher than the type you're used to," Raoul

said, tousling the boy's shaggy head and giving him a mock clip on the chin.

"Why did he come with you?"

"To have a look at you. He's never seen an English girl before. I fancy he expected you to have two heads." He said something to Tino, who appraised Polly for some seconds, grinned and answered.

"What was he saying?" she asked.

"He wants to know if all English girls are so scraggy. His choice of word, not mine. In his opinion you don't compare too favorably with Fiametta."

"Who's Fiametta?"

"The belle of the village, I imagine. The majority of Corsicans admire plumpness."

"I'm desolated," Polly said dryly. "If he's interested you might tell him that he could do with a bit more flesh on his bones."

She tore the sandwich into two and offered a piece to Tino, who glanced uncertainly at Raoul and then seized it eagerly.

"He looks half-starved, poor little wretch," she said.

"He's an orphan and the relatives who look after him aren't too openhanded," Raoul said, before turning away to collect their few belongings from the tower.

While he was gone, Polly and Tino ate their crusts and studied each other. Presently she remembered that there was a boiled sweet in the pocket of her slacks, one that Marisa had given her yesterday morning. She fished it out and handed it to him. It was evidently something new to him and he unwrapped it and put it in his mouth with the air of one taking a chance. After a few sucks, he grinned and looked hopefully at her pocket.

Polly shook her head. "Sorry, that's all I've got."

He seemed to understand this and when she had finished her bread, thrust the bottle at her. After drinking a little Polly went over to the tower. Raoul was just coming out.

"Why did you put that drawing on the door?" she asked.

He ripped it off the nail, crunched it in his palm and

pocketed it. "Just in case you had any callers while I was away. It's the sign of my house."

"Would they have known that?"

He nodded. "It would have saved you explaining what you were doing up here with no visible means of support."

She followed him back to the mule and watched him fasten the knapsack behind the pad of sacking and old blanket that formed a rough saddle. There were no stirrups and she was thinking that riding the animal looked like being more tiring than walking when he produced a length of rope and knotted large loops at either end to form footholds. When these were in place he turned, gripped her by the waist and lifted her onto the mule's back with a clipped instruction to swing her right leg astride.

"Comfortable?"

"I think so," she said dubiously.

He fitted the loops under her insteps, called to Tino, who was peering into the tower, and unhitched the reins. Polly expected him to hand them to her, but he looped them around his forearm and said briefly, "They can be temperamental beasts, particularly with strangers."

Long before they were halfway to the village, Polly was envying Tino who tramped alongside her, occasionally looking up and grinning as if he found the spectacle of an English girl on a mule excessively funny. Riding might save one's feet, she thought, but it didn't spare one's seat. Raoul had not spoken to her since they left the tower, although once when the boy, not looking where he was going, sprawled over a pothole, he turned and said something in *patois*. The rest of the way he strode ahead, his dark head gleaming like a raven's wing in the bright light.

The sun was high when at last the luteous-tiled roofs of the hamlet came into view. As they passed between the houses there were swarthy faces at every window and doorway watching their progress, and Tino was soon joined by a score of other children, all eager to look at the foreign girl who wore trousers like a man and painted her lips with red paste.

The people from whom they were borrowing the motorcycle lived at the far end of the village, and the owner of the machine was busily polishing it up as they approached. Passing the mule's reins to an old man in a black corduroy suit and magenta cummerbund, Raoul went over to speak to the youth.

Watched by the children who had formed a circle around her, Polly managed to ease her leg over the animal's back and slide to the ground. But as soon as her feet touched the ground she had to grab the old man's arm to save herself from falling. A murmur of concern went up and Raoul swung around and strode back to her.

"What's the trouble? Are you ill?"

She shook her head, smiled apologetically at the old man and managed to stand unaided. "No, just stiff, my legs have gone to sleep."

He took her arm. "Try walking."

She did so, wincing as circulation returned. "I'm all right now."

"You'd better rest in the cottage for half an hour."

"No, please, I'd rather go on straight away."

"Sure?"

"Yes, quite." She eyed the pillon on the motorcycle. It looked a little more comfortable than the saddle.

Ten minutes later after saying goodbye to their helpers and a disappointed Tino, they started the last lap of the journey. It took them an hour to reach the castle, and several times the engine spluttered ominously, making Polly fear that they were going to be stranded again. By the time they drew up at the main door she was too hot and parched and weary to think of anything but having a bath and a long cold drink and a rest.

She had hardly dismounted before Tonio and Renata came hurrying down the steps. In a tone that suggested that he was equally fatigued, Raoul told the housekeeper to stop her lamentations and then listened to the steward, who seemed unperturbed by their prolonged absence but anxious to impart some information. After hearing what he had to say, Raoul gave him some instructions and then gestured for Polly to go inside.

But as she turned toward the staircase, he said, "No, wait a moment, I know you're tired, but I want a word with you before you go up to rest. In here."

Too exhausted to argue, she followed him into the study. "Sit down. We could both do with a drink. Don't worry about Marisa. She's out for a walk with a visitor." He busied himself at a cabinet for a moment and then handed her a glass of lime strongly laced with gin. "Get that down. You need it."

Thankful to be able to stretch her legs and lean her head against a cushion, she sipped the drink and waited for whatever it was he wanted to say. Presently, the gin had dissipated some of her tiredness, she realized that he seemed to be having difficulty in expressing himself. He leaned against the big leather-topped desk, studying his own glass of whiskey and soda with a contemplative frown.

At last, turning his back on her, he said, "What happened last night was...a mistake. If you find that a pretty poor excuse, I can scarcely blame you. But if you're wondering how fast you can pack your bags I want you to reconsider."

There was a silence.

"Is that all you want to say?" Polly asked, after a while.

He turned to face her again, his expression closed and unreadable.

"There's nothing more I can say at the moment."

She put her glass aside and pushed herself up from the chair. "All I can think about at the moment is a cold bath," she said, brushing back a lock of hair.

His mouth compressed for a second. Then he said, "You'd better go to bed until dinner. I'm sorry you've had such a rough time."

She opened her mouth to speak, changed her mind and, without looking at him, left the room.

AT FIVE O'CLOCK, unable to bear inactivity a moment longer, Polly got off the bed and took a second bath. Feeling that the evening ahead might in some way be a

crucial one, she spent some time on her hair and face
and then put on a slim button-down dress of deep hya-
cinth linen. As she stepped into her shoes, she wondered
if Giles had heard about their failure to return last night
and, if so, what his reaction was.

Marisa was not in any of the rooms along the corridor, so Polly concluded that she must be out of
doors somewhere. But as she crossed the hall she heard
the child's voice coming from the yellow salon. Supposing that Raoul would be resting and that her charge
was prattling to Prunella and the beloved kitten,
she opened the door and walked in. Too late to re-
treat, she saw that both Raoul and a slim, dark-haired
woman whom she had never seen before were with the
child.

"I thought you were going to rest until dinner,"
Raoul said, getting to his feet.

Conscious that the woman was looking at her with
frank interest, Polly said, "It was too hot to sleep, and
I'm quite rested now."

He gave a slight shrug and then turning to his companion said, "Nicole, this is Polly Linsey. Polly—my
sister, Madame de Castres. She arrived last night and is
going to stay for a few weeks."

"How do you do, Miss Linsey. Raoul has written
about you and I've been looking forward to meeting
you," Nicole de Castres said pleasantly, holding out a
thin hand.

Later, Polly realized that Nicole was really rather
plain, but at first acquaintance she gave the impression
of beauty, partly because of her faultless grooming and
partly because her brown eyes reflected the warmth and
charm of her personality.

"I expect you are wondering where I've sprung
from," she said with a laugh, when they had shaken
hands. "I've always had a weakness for doing everything on the spur of the moment, and the day before
yesterday I suddenly had a bout of homesickness, so I
hopped on a plane for Ajaccio and here I am. How do
you like Corsica, Miss Linsey?"

"It's beautiful. I'm not surprised you miss it," Polly said.

"There was a time when I loathed living here. I couldn't stand the insularity of everyone and was desperately keen to explore the wide world. But I suppose I'm getting old, because I sometimes feel it might be a good idea to come back for good," Nicole said, a shadow seeming to cross her face for an instant. "Raoul has just been telling me about your adventure in the mountains. Rather a horrid one, I would think. I remember that old tower. Did you see the ghost?"

"I didn't know there was one."

"Oh, yes it's supposed to have been the scene of some gory incident."

"I didn't tell you the story because I thought you had enough to contend with," Raoul put in.

For an instant their eyes met, and Polly felt her cheeks growing warm. "Did you have a good journey, madame?" she asked quickly.

"Yes, very good. I wish you would build a landing field and buy a helicopter, Raoul. The drive up from Ajaccio is almost as long as the flight from Paris," Nicole remarked.

Raoul smiled at her. "Inaccessibility has its advantages," he said dryly. "Marisa will you run and ask Constancià for fresh tea? I expect Polly would like some."

"I must say you have done wonders for that child, Miss Linsey," Nicole said when her niece had left the room. "She looks quite different from when I last saw her, poor mite. Raoul was very lucky to find you."

Polly managed a polite smile, wondering how much Madame de Castres knew.

"I expect you are wondering why I did not take care of her after Charles and Nina were killed," the older woman went on. "Under other circumstances I would have loved to have had her—especially as we never had a child ourselves." She paused, twisting the broad gold band on the third finger of her left hand. "My husband was killed just before the others, and for a time I was too wretched to think of anyone else. Afterward I took up my work again and have been too busy to give her my full attention."

"I'm sorry," Polly said quietly.

Nicole spread her hands. "At least I was very happy for five years, that is not given to everyone." Then, dismissing the subject, she said, "Tell me, how do you get on with Raoul? Does he bully you as he used to do me, or do you handle him as well as you obviously do Marisa?"

Polly blushed vividly, and Raoul said, "She certainly won't tell you in front of me, my dear. If you want to catechize her on those lines I had better get out."

Polly heard him get up and walk out onto the terrace. A moment later Constancia arrived with a tea tray.

"I'm sorry. I didn't mean to embarrass you," Nicole said, when the maid had withdrawn. She poured out two cups, then lit a cigarette and settled herself more comfortably in her chair. "I wasn't sure what to expect," she said presently. "Raoul described you in his letter as being very young, very independent and very feminine. I see now what he meant. To be frank it was fifty percent curiosity that brought me here."

"I'm afraid it must seem very irregular," Polly said awkwardly. "Your brother giving me this post without taking up references...or...or anything."

"He just said he'd found you in Cannes.".

"I'm not a...a gold-digger, Madame de Castres," Polly said anxiously.

The older woman laughed with genuine amusement. "My dear, anyone with half an eye could see that at once—and do call me Nicole, won't you. Not that I would be in the least worried if you were, a gold digger, I mean. Raoul is much too experienced to fall into the greedy little clutches of that particular species. Women have been pursuing him since he was in his teens. Some of them for mercenary reasons: others because they found him attractive. He discovered the frailties of our sex at a very early age, I'm afraid." She paused. "You have been very good for him, I imagine."

Polly stared. "I? But we don't...that is, I'm with Marisa most of the time."

"Your father is a doctor, I believe? And you have several brothers and a nice ordinary background?"

"Well, yes, But—"

"That's what I meant. As you know our parents were drowned in a storm when we were children. I was already being educated at a convent school in France and Raoul was sent to a boarding school in England. It was what our father had wanted. He adored my mother and was happy here, but he never lost a sense of exile, I think." She drank some tea and selected a cake, but did not eat it. "So you see, between childhood and early manhood Raoul was more or less cut off from feminine society. When our grandfather died he was just twenty and straight away he had to take over the management of Maranza and the business connections in France. He began to meet women—mostly the kind of women who can be very dangerous to a youth of that age."

Polly tried to imagine Raoul as a boy of twenty and failed. "Yes, I see," she said vaguely.

Nicole smiled. "I doubt if you do, my dear. I don't expect you to have any idea how rapacious and unscrupulous women can be. I spent a week in Cannes with him once and saw the whole range." She made a *moue* of distaste. "The jaded wives looking for someone to amuse them, the girls who would go to any limits for a fur cape or a pair of diamond clips, the nasty old matrons ready to sell their daughters to the highest bidder. Ugh! Human beings can be disgusting sometimes. You are probably the first disinterested girl he has met for years."

"But surely, in Corsica—" Polly began.

"Yes, but it isn't quite the same," Nicole said, guessing what she had been about to say. "Girls are so much more carefully sheltered than in England that they can't offer the same kind of free and easy companionship. You've met Antonetta Rivera, I expect. Raoul had the greatest difficulty in convincing her father that she wouldn't come to any harm in Paris."

At that point Marisa came back and the conversation turned to other subjects. Polly learned that Nicole worked for a firm of public relations consultants, that her husband had been an officer in the French Army, that she lived in an apartment high above the Seine and found relaxation in painting.

Next day Raoul invited several guests, including the Riveras, to dinner. One of them was a quiet gray-haired man in his early forties named Robert Sagone, and it was immediately evident to Polly that his regard for Nicole was deeper than the affection of old friends. Perhaps he had something to do with Nicole's inclination to return to Corsica.

Seated near the head of the table, Antonetta was looking lovelier than ever, her smooth ivory skin set off by a rather daring dress of gold lamé that made her look more sophisticated than usual. Once or twice Polly saw her father looking at his daughter's bare shoulders and low décolletage with a hint of disapproval, and guessed that he would have preferred to see her in something more demure.

In odd moments between responding to the courteous remarks of the men on either side of her, Polly could not help watching the girl and remembering their talk in the garden a few days before. Yet, as Antonetta leaned forward to speak to Raoul, she did not look like a girl elated in the presence of her beloved. Was she clever enough to hide her feelings until she knew they were shared? Or had the importance of modesty and reserve been so impressed upon her since childhood that she would never dream of relaxing her guard until she was formally betrothed? Yet that first day in the hall she had flung herself into Raoul's arms without any trace of shyness or subsequent confusion.

It was about an hour after the meal had ended and the guests were discussing French foreign policy in the yellow salon, when Polly suddenly realized that three people were missing, Raoul and the Riveras. No one else seemed to have noticed their absence, even after they had been gone for nearly half an hour. And then, while

Robert Sagone was holding attention with an amusing story; the door opened and Antonetta slipped quietly in and found a chair. Polly caught her breath. It was plain that Antonetta was moving in a dream. Her eyes were lambent with happiness and her whole face betrayed her joy. A few minutes later her father and Raoul also returned, and although they quickly resumed their parts in the general intercourse, they both looked noticeably pleased.

When the last guests had departed, Nicole sank onto a couch, put up her feet and asked Raoul to make her a mild gin and tonic.

"No, don't run away, Polly. Unless you are aching for bed," she said, as Polly moved toward the door. "You know, I am almost completely decided to come home. The lease of my flat ends in the autumn and I shall have to move out because the owner wants it for a relative. I think later in the week I shall go down to Ajaccio and see if I can find a little house."

Raoul handed her the drink. "There's a house not far from here that would suit you," he said gravely.

She smiled. "Robert's? Perhaps. . . in time."

They chatted for ten minutes, including Polly in the conversation. Then Nicole finished her drink and got up. Raoul saw them to the door and kissed his sister good-night.

He smiled at Polly with unexpected gentleness. "Don't let her keep you gossiping. Good night."

"Good night."

Nicole did not speak as they went upstairs. But at the door of her room she paused. "Perhaps I had a premonition that I was going to be needed here," she said. "It's a long time since there was a wedding at Maranza. Sleep well, my dear."

CHAPTER EIGHT

THE JIGSAW fell neatly and heart-wrenchingly into place. Polly could only marvel that she had not grasped the significance of Raoul's and the Riveras' temporary disappearance earlier. No wonder Antonetta had looked as if she were on the threshold of a private heaven. Very soon there would be another and larger dinner party, perhaps a ball, at which the alliance of the houses of Maranza and Rivera would be officially announced.

Had she been in a country where trains and buses were available at almost every hour of the day and night, Polly would have thrown her possessions together and left immediately. The prospect of staying on at the castle, of being a party to the engagement celebrations and hearing the plans for the wedding, was unendurable. But because this was Corsica and her only means of escape was the old mail bus that lurched into the village at noon each day, she would have to endure it for a time.

At lunchtime the following day Raoul announced that he would have to drive up to Calvi on urgent business and might be away for a couple of nights.

"Must you? Just now?" Nicole asked, looking surprised.

"Yes, I must, unfortunately. Do you want to come?"

"No, I've promised to lunch with Robert tomorrow."

He left the castle at four. Polly watched the Jaguar sweep down the drive, her eyes misted with tears. She pressed her hot forehead against the cool pane and felt misery lying like a dull weight inside her. He had gone. She would never see him again. It was all over.

That night she packed most of her things and wondered how she was going to explain her departure to Marisa. Nicole left for her lunch date with Robert Sagone around ten o'clock in order to pay a short call on other friends en route.

"You look a bit washed out, my dear," she said before she left.

"I do feel a little limp. It's been hotter these last few days," Polly admitted.

Nicole smiled and patted her cheek. "It suits you—the pale and interesting look. I'll be back for dinner."

When she had gone Polly went to find Marisa. On the way she asked Tonio if he would take her down to the village at eleven. She found the child playing on the terrace. Telling her was one of the hardest things she had ever had to do.

"But I thought you were going to stay with me always. Uncle Raoul said so," the little girl said disbelievingly.

"I wish I could, darling. But I have a family of my own, and now that Tante Nicole is here you won't be lonely anymore, will you?" Polly said wretchedly.

"I want you. Tante Nicole is nice, but I want you, Polly."

"Oh, Marisa, you must try to understand. I have to go home. I just have to."

The child did not cry, but the look in her eyes told Polly what she had done.

"But you haven't said goodbye to Uncle Raoul," she said presently in a small disconsolate voice.

"I've written him a note. He will understand." With an effort of will Polly made herself smile and say cheerfully, "Perhaps I'll come back to see you one day."

Marisa gazed at her sorrowfully. "I thought you were going to live here always," she repeated.

At last it was over. As Tonio drove her away in the newly repaired jeep, she looked back and saw the child waving from the steps and had to avert her face so that the steward would not see the tears pouring down her cheeks. As they neared the village, she prayed that Giles would not have gone off on a climbing expedition and was immeasurably relieved when she saw him reading at a table outside the café.

"Polly! What goes on?" he asked when he saw the suitcase in the back of the jeep.

"I'm catching the bus to Ajaccio and flying home," she said briefly.

He saw the traces of tears and heard the quiver in her voice.

"Right, I'll come with you. It won't take me long to pack my gear," he said briskly.

It was not until they were sitting on a bench in the square waiting for the bus to arrive that he said quietly, "Like to tell me what happened?"

She longed to be able to bury her face in his shoulder and weep out her heartbreak. Instead, plucking nervously at her handkerchief, she said, "Nothing much. Raoul's sister arrived from Paris a day or two ago and is planning to settle here, so I may as well get home. It seems ages since I left England."

He forbore to ask any more questions. "Well, we may not be able to get a plane tonight, but I would think there'll be some seats going tomorrow," he said.

The bus was already crowded and Giles had to stand part of the way. It was a slow and uncomfortable journey, but Polly was beyond feeling physical discomforts. She kept seeing Marisa's uncomprehending face and feeling that she had committed a particularly despicable kind of treachery.

It was early evening when they finally rumbled into Ajaccio. Without waiting for her consent Giles hailed a cab to take them around the city until they found rooms. By good fortune the second place they visited had two rooms free, and while Polly was shown upstairs he telephoned the airport to inquire about flights to England. When sometime later he came up to her room, it was with the news that unless they were able to take over cancellations, they would have to wait until the day after next.

"Are you sure?" Polly said anxiously. She had hoped to leave Corsica the following morning.

"Sorry, but it's a busy time of year. I've told them to let us know immediately if anyone backs out at the last moment." He put a hand on her drooping shoulders. "Why don't you have a snack up here and then get straight to bed? You looked fagged out."

She sighed. "Yes, I think I will. Thank you, Giles."

THE FOLLOWING DAY dragged interminably. They spent most of it in the hotel lounge, hoping for a call from the airport, but none came. That evening, when Giles was chatting to a middle-aged Englishman who had just arrived, Polly excused herself and went out for a walk.

She walked for an hour, blind to the lights of the cafés and deaf to the chink of glasses and bursts of laughter. But presently, realizing that Giles might be worried about her and that she ought to return, she stopped and found that she was outside the hotel where Raoul had brought her for tea on her first visit to the city. As she stood there, looking up at the imposing white façade and remembering their talk in the garden while Marisa slept, a taxi drew up and a young couple got out.

"Polly! What are you doing here?"

Polly froze, unable to move or speak.

"Raoul did not say he was coming to Ajaccio today," Antonetta went on. She laughed. "I suppose he was being very discreet." Then, turning to her escort, "Polly, this is my fiancé, Philippe Garde. Philippe, this is Miss Linsey, who came from England to take care of Raoul's niece."

The young man bowed. He was tall and slimly built with curly black hair and happy blue eyes.

"*Enchanté, mademoiselle,*" he said politely.

Polly stared at him blankly. "Your *fiancé!*" she repeated in a strangled voice.

"But yes—I thought you knew! I told you about Philippe, I am sure of it. We were not engaged then because papa did not want me to marry until after my twentieth birthday. But Raoul persuaded him, and so very soon—" with a radiant smile at the young man

"—I shall not be Mademoiselle Rivera but Madame Garde. Oh, Polly, I am so happy!"

Polly swayed slightly and began to laugh. Antonetta looked faintly perplexed, and then, as her fiancé spoke to her in an urgent undertone, she gripped the other girl's arm and said anxiously, "Polly, are you not well? What is the matter?"

Polly drew in a deep breath and managed to control the urge to laugh until she collapsed. She was, she realized, dangerously close to hysteria.

"I'm sorry, Antonetta. I'm very happy for you. Congratulations, Monsieur Garde."

She paused and then said wryly. "You see, Antonetta, that day when you told me about Monsieur Garde, I thought you were talking about Raoul."

"Raoul!" Antonetta looked dumbfounded for a moment, then burst out laughing. "But Raoul is almost old enough to be my father. Well, no, not quite, perhaps, an elder brother. How could you think it was Raoul? Why, he—" She stopped abruptly, puzzlement wrinkling her forehead. "Where is Raoul, Polly?"

Polly passed the back of her hand across her forehead. "In Calvi." She braced her shoulders. "I must go. Goodbye, and good luck."

Then, before they could stop her, she had signaled a passing cab and climbed quickly inside.

When she reached the hotel, she looked through the glass doors of the lounge and saw that Giles was still engrossed in conversation with the other Englishman. Leaving a message for him at the reception desk, she went up to her room and sat down at the table near the double doors that opened onto the balcony. She was still too stunned by Antonetta's revelation of the truth to be capable of logical thought. But after a little her brain began to function again. Raoul was not engaged to Antonetta. He did not love her or want her for his wife, because he had helped her to become engaged to another man. Then what had Nicole meant by her remark that it was a long time since there had been a wedding at Maranza? Was there someone else? No, there couldn't be. For an instant the wildest hope soared inside her, but only for an instant. *If it were that,* she thought, *he would have shown it, have said something.*

A tap at the door heralded Giles bearing a tray of coffee and pastries.

"I thought your walk might have perked up your appetite," he said. "Can I come in and share some?"

"Yes, do. You seemed to be having an enthralling talk when I glanced in on my way up here," she said.

"Yes, I was. Old Fox is a jolly interesting chap once you get him going. How are you feeling? You look a bit down."

"I'm all right."

"Oh, I forgot. We're fixed up for the seats on the morning plane. With any luck we should be back in U.K. this time tomorrow."

"Good. I don't think I could stand much more hanging around."

"You know, I have a feeling that you're holding something back," Giles said slowly. "No, I'm not asking what it is. But if at any time you do want to get something off your chest, don't be shy, will you?"

She smiled and squeezed his hand. "Dear Giles, I think you're the nicest person I know."

"I wish I were so nice that you couldn't do without me," he said with a wry grin. "Come on, get cracking on some of this food. You hardly touched your lunch." He paused. "I wonder if either of us will ever come back here?"

"I won't," Polly said flatly. "After tomorrow Corsica will just be a blob on the map."

"Mm, but I won't forget this holiday," Giles said reflectively. "Apart from everything else, there is something about the place that gets you somehow."

"Don't you wish you'd stayed with your friends and gone to Italy instead?"

"No, it hasn't turned out as I'd hoped, but I don't regret it."

They were both silent for a while, immersed in their own thoughts. Presently Giles asked if he could light his pipe, and as she watched him pressing tobacco into the bowl, Polly thought that he would probably end up as a surgeon like his father. His strong sensitive fingers were made for the precise art of surgery.

"So this is where you hide yourself," said a voice from the door.

"*Raoul!*" Polly's hand flew to her cheek and she half rose from her chair, every drop of color draining from her face, her eyes dilated with shock and alarm.

He closed the door and leaned against it. "Surprised?" he asked softly.

She swallowed, fighting down panic. "I t-thought you were in Calvi," she stammered.

"I got away sooner than I expected." Then he said, without taking his eyes off her, "Would you leave us for a few minutes, Barrington? I have some private business to discuss with Miss Linsey."

Giles, who was looking both puzzled and annoyed by this unexpected and unannounced intrusion, opened his mouth to reply. But before he could do so, Polly said quickly, "No! Don't go, Giles."

"But if St. Clair wants—"

Struggling to retain some measure of calm, Polly sat down and in a carefully controlled voice said, "Please stay, Giles."

"Are you sure you want an audience?" Raoul asked from the door.

She kept her eyes on the table. "I have no secrets from Giles."

"But, Polly, if it's private—" Giles began.

Raoul cut him short. "I fancy she feels in need of moral support, Barrington," he said derisively.

Giles looked bewilderedly from one to the other. "Look here, what *is* all this about?" he asked uncomfortably.

"Precisely what I've come to find out," Raoul said coolly. "Well, Miss Linsey?"

Polly's hands, hidden below the table, clenched convulsively.

"I don't know what you're talking about," she said frigidly.

He laughed, and it was not a pleasant sound. "It's simple enough. I merely want to know why you left Maranza so suddenly. It's usual to give notice before one leaves employment, I believe."

"But, Polly, you said that—" Giles began perplexedly.

"I know. I'm sorry, Giles. I didn't want to lie to you," she said wretchedly. "You see, I thought that—"

This time it was he who broke in. "Didn't you know that I would understand anything you did?" he said gently.

"Oh, yes, it wasn't that." She gave him a quick agonized glance and then averted her face, trying desperately to think of some way out of this appalling situation.

"Perhaps she felt that the truth might impel you to do me some violence," Raoul said sardonically.

Giles swung around to face him the puzzlement on his face giving place to a look of indignant suspicion.

"Now look here, St. Clair, I don't know what the devil's been going on that Polly hasn't told me, but if you've done anything to hurt her I'll—"

"You'll what? Challenge me to a duel? Kick me down the stairs?" Raoul inquired silkily, surveying Giles's shorter, stockier figure with insolent amusement.

The younger man's fair skin flushed with angry color and his fists doubled. He took a suggestive pace forward, but before he could advance farther, Polly jumped up and clutched his arm.

"No, Giles! Don't let him provoke you. This has nothing to do with you."

"Perhaps it hasn't. But I'm damned if I'll stand by and watch this...this oaf browbeat you," he said furiously.

"Very chivalrous of you, but a trifle rash," Raoul said mockingly. He was still leaning against the door, hands in pockets, and his casual stance and the glint of derision in his eyes were calculated to incense.

But as Giles brushed off her restraining hand and took another step forward, Polly's temper flared.

"Stop it, both of you!" she exlaimed. "I've had just about as much as I can stand. If you let him goad you into a fight, Giles. I'll never speak to you again."

Giles wavered. Then reluctantly he relaxed.

"But Polly—" he started.

"No, let me deal with him," she said hastily, "I've brought this on myself. I should have known it would happen."

"Yes, if you'd realized that earlier it would have saved me an unnecessary drive and averted this interview," Raoul agreed.

She swung to face him, her eyes sparkling with anger, her chin lifted proudly.

"You weren't obliged to come, Mr. St. Clair," she said icily.

"No, but I don't care for people walking out on me without an explanation. If you thought I'd swallow that pack of nonsense in your letter, you overestimated my credulity."

"No, I didn't think you would," she admitted evenly. "But I thought the real reason would be obvious enough. I've never been under any obligation to give you formal notice, and if you want to know why I left while you were away—it was because I couldn't rely on your letting me go otherwise. Well, you may have a feudal kind of authority in Maranza, but it doesn't apply here in Ajaccio, and nothing you can do or say will make me go back."

His eyes narrowed. "Are you sure of that?"

Polly did not flinch. "Perfectly sure," she returned crisply.

He regarded her speculatively for a moment. "Has your stay in Corsica been such a wretched one?"

She tried to hold his glance, but something in the keen blue eyes made her own falter.

"No, not wretched exactly," she said in a low voice. "But I've been here long enough. It's time I went home."

"Corsica could be that if you wanted it."

She stiffened, her heart missing a beat. "W-what do you mean?"

He shrugged and moved past her toward the balcony. "I had an idea that you rather liked the island now. You said something once about it casting a spell over people," he said without expression.

"Did I? I don't remember."

"Marisa is very upset about your going. She's been crying her eyes out ever since you left."

Polly's mouth trembled. "Oh, please—you're not being fair," she said distressfully.

He turned. "Fair! Do you think it's fair to make a child fond of you then walk out at a moment's notice? Is it fair to accept responsibilities and then throw them aside at the drop of a hat?"

"Really, St. Clair, you've no right to take that tone with her," Giles objected, putting a protective arm around Polly's shoulders and glaring at him.

"You keep out of this. She's not a schoolgirl. She can answer for herself," Raoul said savagely.

Polly felt Giles's arm tighten and saw his jaw set.

"He's right," she said tonelessly. "I'm not a schoolgirl, and if he insists on the whole truth, he'd better have it. Would you leave us for a little while, Giles?"

"No, I won't," Giles said ferociously. "He's got no right to barge in here and throw his weight around. I never approved of you staying in that damned mausoleum, and if I'd known you were being treated like this I'd have got you out of it long ago." Then he said to Raoul, "Now stop pestering the girl and get out, or I'll call the police and have you chucked out."

"Giles, please! It won't help matters to have a public scene. Just give me five minutes. I'll call you if I need you," she said persuasively.

"But, Polly—"

"Please!"

"Oh, very well, if that's the way you want it. But—" with a dark glance at Raoul "—I'll be in the corridor if you want help."

"Thank you." She managed a wan smile and squeezed his arm gratefully. As soon as he had gone, she drew a deep breath and forced herself to meet Raoul's eyes again, finding them curiously somber.

"It must be a novel experience—to have your wishes flouted," she said dryly. "Did you really think you could force me to go back?"

He lit a cigarette and flipped the spent match into a plant pot. For the first time she noticed how tired he looked, tired and oddly drawn.

"I hoped to take you back, but not by force."

She raised her eyebrows. "By the same methods you used the last time, I suppose."

"You'll never forgive me for that, will you? Even though it turned out to be perfectly respectable."

"I prefer to go into things with my eyes open," she said, coldly. "You can't have it your way all the time, Mr. St. Clair."

"For God's sake stop calling me Mr. St. Clair in that prim voice," he snapped at her. "You called me Raoul quite happily until I left, and as far as I know nothing has happened to change that. Now what is all this about? Why did you duck out the minute my back was turned?"

"Because I wanted to. Isn't that reason enough?"

"No, by heaven, it isn't. You were never forced to stay. You could have left at any moment you chose. But for some obscure reason you had to sneak away like an escaping prisoner. I want to know that reason."

"I've told you. I . . . I'm tired of Corsica. I want to go home to England."

"Where you'll settle down with Barrington in some peaceful suburb and try to forget that you ever set foot here, I suppose," he said sarcastically.

"I don't know what Giles plans to do. I shall get another job."

"D'you mean you're not going to marry him after all?"

"I never said I was."

"Not in so many words, perhaps, but the implication was fairly strong."

She did not reply and after a moment he said, "You've always been afraid of me, haven't you?"

"Afraid? No, I don't think so—although I've had reason to be at times," she said coolly.

He made an impatient gesture. "I didn't mean that sort of fear. You've been frightened of this thing between us."

"W-what 'thing'?"

He smiled then, and she had to look away because his smile had so often been her undoing.

"The eleventh hour, and you're still determined to ignore it," he said with a sound that was something between exasperation and amusement. "Or have you really no idea why we clash so frequently?"

"Because we're fundamentally incompatible, I suppose," she said dully.

He brought the flat of his hand onto the table with a force that made the glasses ring. "Don't lie! You know it isn't that."

Her chin came up again, but she could not control the violent trembling that seized her.

"What do you want me to say?"

When he spoke his voice was quiet again and slightly husky.

"For once in your ostrich existence, I want you to face the truth. If you honestly believe that the feelings that you've been at such pains to suppress boil down to nothing more than antagonism—well, I still won't be convinced but I'll accept it. But be very sure you aren't deluding yourself, little one." He paused and she saw the muscles at his jaw working. "I'm asking you to marry me, Polly."

For a full minute there was an electric silence.

"To marry you!" she whispered faintly. *"To marry you!"*

"Is it really so astounding?"

She felt for the chair behind her and dropped into it, her legs weak.

"You can't be serious! There are a hundred nurses—a thousand—who will jump at the job. Marisa may be upset for a day or two, but she'll soon get used to someone else. It...it's fantastic to go to such lengths."

"My God, are you really such a nincompoop that you think I'd marry you to keep your professional services! To the devil with Marisa—and everyone else, I want you for my wife—nothing else, just my wife. Can't you get it into your thick little head? I love you!"

Polly stared at him. Was this really happening? Had he really said the longed-for words? Or was she suffering from some form of delirium?

"I'll give you half an hour to make up your mind," Raoul said. "Either you come with me now, or the sooner you leave Corsica the better for both of us. If you decide to come with me, I'll be waiting in the car across the road." He glanced at his watch. "It's half-past nine. I shall leave at ten."

He turned and moved to the door. Then with his fingers on the handle, he paused and looked at her. "I love you very much, Polly," he said quietly.

When, a few moments later, Giles returned, he found Polly still standing where Raoul had left her.

"What is it?" he said anxiously. "What happened? Polly, you must tell me."

"Nothing. Everything. Oh, Giles...." Suddenly she was crying against his shoulder.

"The swine!" Giles fumed, patting her back. "That rotten—"

"Oh, no, you don't understand." She had difficulty in speaking and her eyes glimmered with tears, but as she raised her face he saw she was transfigured. "He loves me. He wants to marry me. He's given me half an hour to make up my mind. Oh, Giles, I can't believe it."

"I see." He drew away and then gave her his handkerchief.

After a little while Polly recovered herself. "I'm sorry. It must be a shock to you. I didn't mean to blurt it out like that. Oh, Giles, what a beast you must think me."

He looked at her, and she read the pain in his eyes and ached with compassion for him. She knew so well what this meant to him.

"No, I don't," he said gruffly. "I think I had an inkling some time ago. Are you sure, Polly? Absolutely sure?"

"Yes, absolutely sure."

"Then you'd better not waste any time. Want a hand?"

She shook her head, her throat thick.

"If you don't mind I think I'll say goodbye," he said. "You will be all right?"

"Of course." He managed a crooked grin. "You're not the only pebble on the beach, you know. This time next year I may be thanking my stars you wouldn't have me. Take care of yourself."

For the briefest fraction of time she felt his arms around her and his lips against her cheek, and then he was gone. Listening to footsteps receding down the corridor, she prayed that his brave boast would come true, that this time next year he would have found someone else.

When, at five minutes to ten, she took her case from the porter, tipped him, and looked across the road to the Jaguar, Raoul was not behind the wheel. He was pacing up and down the pavement behind the car. As she watched him, he dropped a cigarette on the path and ground it out with his heel. Then he saw her.

They met in the middle of the road.

"You cut it rather fine, didn't you?" he said tersely, taking her case.

"I had to. . .to explain to Giles, and to pack."

He gave her that oddly brilliant glance that she had never been able to fathom, and then, without speaking, put her into the car and locked her case in the trunk. Thirty seconds later they were away.

Soon the town was left behind and they were roaring up into the dark hills. She had no very clear idea of how far they had gone when, so suddenly that she had to grab the armrest, he trod on the brake, geared down and swung off the road onto a patch of bumpy ground around a group of pines. For a few moments after they had come to a standstill he sat very still staring through the windscreen. Then switching off the engine and head-lights, he leaned back and she heard him let out a sigh.

"Well now," he said, "suppose we find out why it took us so long to get to this point. No, on second thought, we'll leave the postmortem for a bit. After the twenty-five minutes of purgatory you gave me, I'm in no mood to be reasonable. Ye gods, when I got back from Calvi and found you'd done a bolt, I. . . ."

The rest was lost as he reached out and drew her into his arms, burying his face in her hair. For a while he was content to hold her close, and then his fingers found her chin and he tipped up her face. This time his kisses were gentle and Polly did not resist.

Sometime later, her head on his shoulder, Polly said tremulously, "But, Raoul, I don't understand."

"That makes two of us. What's your particular puzzle, my love?"

"Almost everything. If. . .if you felt like this, why didn't you tell me?"

"How could I when I thought you were more than half in love with Barrington? That night at the tower—"

"But I wanted you to kiss me. I wanted it more than anything in the world," she told him.

"One would never have guessed it," he said dryly. "You fought me off like a young tigress."

"Because I knew—or thought I knew—that Antonetta loved you and that you were planning to marry her."

"Antonetta! My sweet idiot, you obviously need your head examined. Antonetta's crazy about a dashing young sprig she met in Paris, and as far as I'm concerned she's just a pretty kid whom I've know since she was knee high to a grasshopper. What, in heaven's name, put that mad notion into your silly little noddle?"

Polly explained as best as she could while he was caressing the curve of her cheek with his fingertips.

"And besides, I'm so unsuitable—not a bit the sort of person you ought to. . .to. . ." she concluded.

"To love as I never thought I could love a woman?" he asked softly, his lips against her forehead. "Kiss me, Polly. Tell me you mean this, that you won't try to slip away from me again."

She slid her arms over his shoulders. "I love you," she whispered, "I love you so much. I'll never want to leave you."

He strained her against him. "You won't get the chance. I'll never let you go now."

"But when. . .?"

"Did I fall in love with you? That night at the club in Cannes when they dressed you up like a trollop and you still managed to look as if you'd strayed out of the schoolroom."

"So if I hadn't met Ginette all this would never have happened?"

"I expect you'd have been happy enough with someone else," he said teasingly.

She clung to him. "But not like this! Never like this!"

"Are you very sure, my heart? Corsica is a long way from England and there'll be times when you'll miss all the familiar things."

"You are everything I shall ever want now."

He took her face between his hands and looked deep into her eyes.

"And you are everything a man could dream of, my dear love," he told her huskily before his lips found hers.

It was growing light when they neared Maranza. Tired but blissfully happy, Polly had fallen asleep in Raoul's arms and woken to find him also sleeping. Now, as they drove over the hill above the village and she saw the castle towering above the sleeping village, her heart lifted and she felt that all the years of her life had been a preparation for this moment of exquisite joy.

As the sun rose from beyond the sea, the great white peak of Monte d'Oro was tinted with a rosy luster and the dawn breeze fanning her cheek was sweeter than wine. Mimosa, tamarisk, oleander, wild mint and juniper—they were a rich exchange for the flowers of her homeland, she thought contentedly.

"Happy?" Raoul asked, his eyes so tender that her heart skipped a beat.

She slipped her hand through his arm and slid closer. "Deliriously," she said.

FIVE DAYS LATER Polly sat in an airplane and watched the sea falling away below her. As she moved her left hand a dazzle of brilliant green light was reflected in the thick pane at her elbow. She looked down at the big square-cut emerald on her third finger. Although she had been wearing it since the day of her return to Maranza, she could still scarcely believe that it belonged to her and was terrified of losing it. Somehow the costly stone with its border of tiny diamonds set in platinum seemed too magnificent an adornment for her small capable hands with their short pink nails.

"Excited, *mignonne*?"

She turned to Raoul who was sitting beside her, and as always when he looked at her with that special warmth, her breath caught.

"Yes, terribly. So much has happened since I left home."

His blue eyes glinted and she knew that if they had been alone he would have taken her in his arms. As it was he found her hand and held it hard in his brown strong one.

"I have to convince your parents that I'm a suitable husband before we can be perfectly sure of the future."

"I'm over twenty-one. You can't make that an excuse to jilt me," Polly said, laughing. Then said, seriously, "I know they'll like you at once."

"I shall have to find some way of repaying my debt to Andrew," he said.

"To Drew? What debt?"

"If you hadn't had that sos from him, you might never have come home with me."

She smiled, thinking how easily happiness could be missed. She could even think kindly of the Vanhassons now, for they, too, had played a part in leading her toward her destiny. Soon—as soon as possible, Raoul had said—she would be married, and after the wedding they were going to spend a long sun-drenched honeymoon on the *Corsair*. And after that there would be all the rest of her life to live. Not, as she had feared, alone, with only her work to bring fulfillment, but in a deep close partnership with the man who she had tried to hate and only succeeded in loving more than life itself.

SPECIAL

Harlequin Romance Treasury Book Offer

This superb Romance Treasury is yours at little or <u>no</u> cost.

3 exciting, full-length Romance novels in one beautiful hard-cover book.

Introduce yourself to Harlequin Romance Treasury. The most beautiful books you've ever seen!

Cover and spine of each volume features a distinctive gilt design.
An elegant bound-in ribbon bookmark completes the classic design.
No detail has been overlooked to make Romance Treasury
volumes as beautiful and lasting as the stories they contain.
What a delightful way to enjoy the very best and most popular
Harlequin romances again and again!

Here's how to get your volume NOW!

Let Your Imagination Fly Sweepstakes

Rules and Regulations:

NO PURCHASE NECESSARY

1. Enter the Let Your Imagination Fly Sweepstakes 1, 2 or 3 as often as you wish. Mail each entry form separately bearing sufficient postage. Specify the sweepstake you wish to enter on the outside of the envelope. Mail a completed entry form or, your name, address, and telephone number printed on a plain 3''x 5'' piece of paper to:

HARLEQUIN LET YOUR IMAGINATION FLY SWEEPSTAKES,

P.O. BOX 1280, MEDFORD, N.Y. 11763 U.S.A.

2. Each completed entry form must be accompanied by l Let Your Imagination Fly proof-of-purchase seal from the back inside cover of specially marked Let Your Imagination Fly Harlequin books (or the words "Let Your Imagination Fly" printed on a plain 3''x 5'' piece of paper. Specify by number the Sweepstakes you are entering on the outside of the envelope.

3. The prize structure for each sweepstake is as follows:

Sweepstake 1 – North America

Grand Prize winner's choice: a one-week trip for two to either Bermuda; Montreal, Canada; or San Francisco. 3 Grand Prizes will be awarded (min. approx. retail value $1,375. U.S. based on Chicago departure) and 4,000 First Prizes: scarves by nik nik, worth $14. U.S. each. All prizes will be awarded.

Sweepstake 2 – Caribbean

Grand Prize winner's choice: a one-week trip for two to either Nassau, Bahamas; San Juan, Puerto Rico; or St. Thomas, Virgin Islands. 3 Grand Prizes will be awarded. (Min. approx. retail value $1,650. U.S., based on Chicago departure) and 4,000 First Prizes: simulated diamond pendants by Kenneth Jay Lane, worth $15. U.S. each. All prizes will be awarded.

Sweepstake 3 – Europe

Grand Prize winner's choice: a one-week trip for two to either London, England; Frankfurt, Germany; Paris, France; or Rome, Italy. 3 Grand Prizes will be awarded. (Min. approx. retail value $2,800. U.S., based on Chicago departure) and 4,000 First Prizes: 1/2 oz. bottles of perfume, BLAZER by Anne Klein. (Retail value over $30. U.S.) All prizes will be awarded.

Grand trip prizes will include coach round-trip airfare for two persons from the nearest commercial airport serviced by Delta Air Lines to the city as designated in the prize, double occupancy accommodation at a first-class or medium hotel, depending on vacation, and $500. U.S. spending money. Departure taxes, visas, passports, ground transportation to and from airports will be the responsibility of the winners.

4. To be eligible, Sweepstakes entries must be received as follows:

Sweepstake 1 Entries received by February 28, 1981
Sweepstake 2 Entries received by April 30, 1981
Sweepstake 3 Entries received by June 30, 1981
Make sure you enter each Sweepstake separately since entries will not be carried forward from one Sweepstake to the next.

The odds of winning will be determined by the number of entries received in each of the three sweepstakes. Canadian residents, in order to win any prize, will be required to first correctly answer a time-limited skill-testing question, to be posed by telephone, at a mutually convenient time.

5. Random selections to determine Sweepstake 1, 2 or 3 winners will be conducted by Lee Krost Associates, an independent judging organization whose decisions are final. Only one prize per family, per sweepstake. Prizes are non-transferable and non-refundable and no substitutions will be allowed. Winners will be responsible for any applicable federal, state and local taxes. Trips must be taken during normal tour periods before June 30, 1982. Reservations will be on a space-available basis. Airline tickets are non-transferable, non-refundable and non-redeemable for cash.

6. The Let Your Imagination Fly Sweepstakes is open to all residents of the United States of America and Canada, (excluding the Province of Quebec) except employees and their immediate families of Harlequin Enterprises Ltd., its advertising agencies, Marketing & Promotion Group Canada Ltd. and Lee Krost Associates, Inc., the independent judging company. Winners may be required to furnish proof of eligibility. Void wherever prohibited or restricted by law. All federal, state, provincial and local laws apply.

7. For a list of trip winners, send a stamped, self-addressed envelope to:

Harlequin Trip Winners List, P.O. Box 1401, MEDFORD, N.Y. 11763 U.S.A.

Winners lists will be available after the last sweepstake has been conducted and winners determined.

NO PURCHASE NECESSARY
